JUNGLE CRAW

The Black Eagles h uitage over the raiders. The VC were in a hurry and had to complete their work before dawn. The Black Eagles had all day. Each man, acting independently, spread out from the others. By staying low and crawling at a steady pace, they could glance up into the night sky and catch the floating silhouettes of the VC around them. With plenty of ammo, and the M16s set on full automatic, they were ready to do more battle than the enemy had expected.

The Falcon eased forward along the ground, alternating quick, darting glances with pressing his ear to the earth for the tell-tale vibrations of running feet. He sensed movement close by and glanced in that direction. Three figures. He waited until they were a mere fifteen feet away, then brought up the muzzle of his weapon. He cut loose two fire-bursts and – in the milliseconds of light afforded by the shots – caught the satisfying sight of the trio of VC staggering back under the impact. He listened for groans, but heard none.

The Falcon went back to his low, slow crawl . . .

Also by John Lansing in Sphere Books:

HANOI HELLGROUND
NIGHTMARE IN LAOS

The Black Eagles 2
Mekong Massacre

JOHN LANSING

SPHERE BOOKS LIMITED
London and Sydney

First published in Great Britain by
Sphere Books Ltd 1985
30-32 Gray's Inn Road, London WC1X 8JL

First published in the United States of America by
Zebra Books, 1983

TRADE
MARK

Set in Times

Printed and bound in Great Britain by
Collins, Glasgow

Dedicated to:
Detachment 2, Company B
17th Special Forces Group (Airborne)
United States Army Reserves
and
Others who unassed the Big Iron Birds with them
back in the early 1960s

Special acknowledgement to:

William L. Fieldhouse and Patrick E. Andrews

The author wishes to express gratitude to Lancer Militaria of Sims, Arkansas for the accurate and speedy service of shipping the materials used in much of the research for this book.

The Black Eagles 2
Mekong Massacre

ONE

Sunlight exploded in the face of the prisoner when the door to the metal box was jerked open. He turned his head away from the unexpected glare and put both hands over his eyes.

'Outside! Outside!' the guard commanded in his shrill voice. 'Outside! Outside!'

The prisoner painfully sat up and struggled to pull his six feet, four-inch body out of the five and a half foot long iron coffin that had been his home for the previous one hundred and twenty hours. He was too stiff and slow to suit the guard, who displayed his displeasure by striking the captive hard across the knees with a heavy wooden truncheon.

Grimacing against the pain and rage, the prisoner stepped out and stood in the blast furnace heat of the tropical afternoon. Despite the hundred plus degrees of temperature and the high humidity, it was a relief to him after the smothering confines he had endured for so long. He was a tall, slim man in his early forties. His hair, though growing out now, gave evidence of always being kept close-cropped and manageable. The two-week growth of beard he sported was definitely not a personal preference on his part. Nor was the dried feces on his legs that had resulted from continual confinement in the horrible box. And standing stark naked in the blazing sun was another torment he bore not from chance but from circumstance. A physical fitness buff before his imprisonment, the prisoner's body was still muscular and supple, his confinement not yet of sufficient duration to bring on deterioration.

'You go to flag!' the guard commanded.

The prisoner had been through this routine before. He stumbled across the prison yard with the guard pushing him occasionally until he stood in front of a tall bamboo pole.

'Look up!' the guard instructed him.

The prisoner dutifully tipped his head back and opened his eyes to see a red banner sporting a large gold star.

'Salute flag!'

The prisoner raised his hand to his brow, then continued the motion until his arm was extended above his head, his fist clenched. Then he sprung out the middle finger and jabbed it at the banner.

'Imperialist dog!' The truncheon slammed into the prisoner's kidneys, knocking him to the ground. 'Get on feet!'

This new ache in his lower back pulsated with the old pains already there as he laboriously re-assumed a standing position.

'Salute flag!'

'Wait.' The voice came from a short distance away.

The prisoner looked in that direction and saw two short oriental men approaching. One wore a khaki uniform with a sun helmet, and the other a nondescript blue Chinese Mao-style type uniform. The latter spoke to the prisoner in a kindly voice. 'Ah, Colonel Baldwin. How can I help you, if you won't cooperate with the prison staff?' The English was correct and barely accented.

'I've asked you for none,' Baldwin said.

'But I *want* to help you,' the man said. 'It is so useless for you to suffer in order to avoid doing a simple, physical act. All you are being asked to do is to raise your hand to your forehead.'

'There's a hell of a lot more to it than that, Doctor Yoon,' Baldwin insisted.

Yoon displayed a disappointed expression. 'Why do you refuse my friendship?' He was a small delicate man, with kindly eyes and sincere, but toothy smile. He sported the wispy moustache typical of middle-aged Oriental men.

'I find it hard to believe that you came all the way from North Korea simply to become friends with me.'

'But, my dear Colonel Baldwin, I most certainly did,' Yoon said. 'That is my sole purpose of being here – to be your friend and guide you through your re-education.'

Baldwin remained silent.

The other man, a North Vietnamese colonel named Nguyen, snorted his displeasure. 'A very bad American. He needs much training to take away his *bourgeois* attitude.' He was the opposite of his companion in physical appearance. Rugged and husky, his face displayed an athletic quality as did the way he moved. Long years of hard soldiering in brutal, unforgiving circumstances had produced a dedicated, tough individual who looked upon physical discomfort and pain as a challenge.

Yoon turned to Nguyen. 'May I ask you a favor, please?'

'Of course, comrade.'

'Give me another chance to work with Colonel Baldwin. I am positive I can change his viewpoint.'

Nguyen shook his head. 'No! We have given this American several opportunities to see the light, but he is stubborn. Only physical punishment will open his eyes.'

'Please, Colonel Nguyen. He hasn't been here a month yet. And I will lose face if I fail with him. Colonel Baldwin is an intelligent man wrapped in the dark cloak of capitalistic ignorance,' Yoon pleaded. 'It will take time to peel away the layers of western decadence.'

Nguyen thought for several moments. 'One more chance then. But no more – no more!'

'Thank you so much, comrade.' Yoon turned to Baldwin. 'Am I not your friend then? You will not have to return to that horrible box.'

Despite his gut feelings, Baldwin felt a surge of gratitude toward the North Korean. For a brief moment he even considered asking for the use of the shower facilities, but quickly reconsidered. Instead, the pilot remained silent.

'But he will get no clothing until he salutes the flag of the people of North Vietnam,' Nguyen said.

Yoon gave Baldwin an imploring look. 'Salute the flag. Please, Colonel Baldwin.'

Silence.

Nguyen barked some terse orders in Vietnamese, and the guard grabbed Baldwin's arm, hustling him across the yard to the block of cells on the far side of the compound.

Lieutenant Colonel Winston Baldwin, United States Air Force, was the unwilling guest of the North Vietnamese in that summer of 1964 through his extraordinary devotion to duty. As the operations officer of a clandestine reconnaissance squadron, this veteran of both World War II in Europe and the Korean War was not the type to be content with sitting behind a desk while directing the highly classified activities of his unit. Baldwin's basic philosophy of military leadership was that a man can't lead, direct or advise missions in which he doesn't actively participate, at least now and then.

His unit was the vanguard of a possible escalation of the American effort to aid the South Vietnamese in their struggle against aggression from the north. Their basic mission was aerial monitoring of activities by the Communists near the border between the two countries.

It was during an overflight of the North Vietnamese jungles that a newly established, hidden SAM site had sent up the missile that punched into Baldwin's RF-4C Phantom. He bailed out over unfriendly territory, his parachute carrying him into tall trees that ripped the nylon canopy to shreds causing him to fall the last fifteen feet and badly twist both ankles.

With only the barest of survival gear, he limped off into the jungle using a lensatic compass to keep him moving on a southerly course. But due to the density of the vegetation, swamps and other impassable terrain features, Baldwin found himself constantly having to backtrack. His progress was further impeded by the proximity of search parties looking for the pilot who had left the shredded parachute behind. Each day without adequate food – and drinking untreated water – began to take its toll until the onslaught of heatstroke felled him.

It was to his credit that he successfully evaded North Vietnamese army patrols for two weeks before he finally collapsed and was discovered by a young soldier who had stepped off a narrow jungle trail to defecate.

A painstaking study of various orders of battle of the United States Air Force by his captors failed to turn up Baldwin's name on any of the usual American air squadrons in the Far East. Further probing proved futile in this unusual situation. It was found necessary to call in Russian intelligence. Within a week, the North Vietnamese knew they had the operations officer of a joint USAF-CIA unit in their hands – and a carefully planned program of interrogation and mind control was launched against the American officer.

His relative high rank and unusual mission gained him admittance to a special prison camp – known officially within the communist hierarchy as Garrison Three – run by Colonel Nguyen Chi Roi, North Vietnam's premier interrogator and warden. And, with the growing activity of the Americans in the south, Nguyen's staff had been supplemented by a North Korean brainwashing expert, Doctor Yoon Hwan, who had developed his skill working on American POWs during the Korean conflict a dozen years earlier.

Baldwin examined his new cell. Part of a square cement building, his quarters measured six feet across, eight feet deep and seven feet tall. There was an iron bunk attached to the wall that was designed by small orientals to accommodate others of their ilk. A thin, straw mattress covered it. Baldwin noted the small chamber pot in one corner of the cell. He considered that the best improvement of his conditions.

Baldwin settled down as best he could on his small bed. He lay quietly, closing his eyes trying to rest up for whatever ordeal awaited him in the near future. He found his nap interrupted by a scraping and tapping noise, as if being done by someone on the far side of the cell wall. He gritted his teeth in anger. Another harassing ploy, no doubt, to add to the discomfort of Yoon's subtle program of promoting mental anguish by degrees.,

The noise continued. Baldwin noticed the irregularity, and this puzzled him. The best way to annoy someone would be to keep up a persistent unceasing rhythm. After a half hour, the true meaning of the noise leaped into his mind.

The Morse code!

The taps were dots and the scrapes were dashes. Baldwin put his ear against the wall where the sound seemed to be coming from. He caught the letters Y-T-O-N – then silence.

Baldwin frantically looked around his cell for something to talk back with. He had seen no other prisoners since his confinement, but that could have been because of his spending most of the time in that black box. Even if it were a trick, it was certainly worth finding out about. He noticed a chipped area on the wall. He got the chamber pot and eased up to the bars in the door for a quick look. As best as he could determine there was no guard close by. He gently struck the wall with the pot until a piece of cement was dislodged, then he went back to his bunk and began his own tapping and scraping.

B-A-L-D-W-I-N – U-S-A-F

He repeated it three times, then waited. The answer came back immediately.

D-A-Y-T-O-N – S-S-G – U-S – A-R-M-Y

Despite his misgivings, Baldwin smiled to himself, and tapped out a question.

W-H-A-T – S-S-G.

The unknown man tapped, S-T-A-F-F – S-G-T

Baldwin was immediately suspicious, then he recalled that the army used a three-letter system of abbreviation for ranks. He decided to do the same for his own grade. He tapped back, L-C-L

H-O-W-D-Y – S-I-R

Baldwin grinned at the display of military courtesy. He tapped: H-O-W – L-O-N-G – Y-O-U – H-E-R-E

W-H-A-T – D-A-T-E was asked.

Baldwin answered: J-U-L – 6-4

1-8 – M-O-N-T-H-S

'Jesus Christ!' Baldwin exclaimed involuntarily. But before he could tap out another message, the sergeant named Dayton sent another.

S-A-L-U-T-E – F-L-A-G

N-O – W-A-Y, Baldwin said.

S-T-A-Y – H-E-A-L-T-H-Y – pause – G-E-T — C-L-O-T-H-E-S another pause G-E-T – B-E-T-T-E-R – C-H-O-W

N-O – F-U-C-K-I-N-G – S-A-L-U-T-E, Baldwin insisted.

The advice came back, L-I-S-T-E-N – T-O – O-L-D – S-A-R-G-E

I – T-H-I-N-K – A-B-O-U-T – I-T, Baldwin told him. He followed this with H-O-W – M-A-N-Y – P-R-I-S-O-N-E-R-S – H-E-R-E

W-I-T-H – Y-O-U – N-O-W – F-I-V-E, the other man responded.

Baldwin surmised that with only that small number of people confined in such a large area, he was being held in a very special place.

The two were able to keep up their scrape-tapping communications for another hour before the activity of the guards caused a cessation in the exchanges. Baldwin lay back on his bunk and pondered the new development. If the man were a genuine prisoner like himself, they might be able to work out something together, if only some morale-raising mutual support. On the other hand, it could be Doctor Yoon sitting on the other side of the wall laughing his ass off.

Only time would tell, but Baldwin did like the advice he got: STAY HEALTHY. That made sense and he did need all the strength he could muster if he were to ever get the hell away from that hellhole. And that he must do. It was of the utmost importance that he not break down under torture or mental harassment.

Baldwin had no choice. It was either that or suicide.

TWO

There was a section of Saigon that was unique even for the exotic city. Although not an actual political department or zone, it had its own name: *Le Quartier des Colons*.

Here were the voluntary expatriates of metropolitan France. Many had gone back to France once, but after years in the colonial service, they discovered they were strangers too far removed from old customs and traditions to become regular Frenchmen again. They were *colons* – now and forever.

These individuals lived in the past – a time of colonial grandeur and authority, when they were the rulers of this humid, hot land. Most of them were only a step or two above poverty – in fact, the ones that were the best off were the retired bureaucrats living on their pensions. The rest had minor jobs in the South Vietnamese government or ran their own businesses – none too lucrative.

The taxi pulled up to the narrow street leading into the *Quartier des Colons*. Two men got out – one a short, stocky Vietnamese, and the other a rangy American named Clayton Andrews. The latter was the CIA case officer for MACV/SOG, the super secret special operations group. Andrews' job could best be described as directing activities into places where angels feared to tread. His companion, a real hard case, was a colonel in the South Vietnamese police who worked directly under all-powerful General Nguyen Ngoc Loan. His name was Tran Hoc – the politest way to reveal his profession would be to say that he was a personality specialist.

The two walked down the narrow street without speaking. The only communication between them was when Tran pointed to a small bistro that bore a faded painted sign which sported the name La Coloniale. They paused at the entrance.

'Careful, aren't they?' Andrews remarked at the double layer of heavy mesh screen that covered the windows.

'A professional, Mister Andrews,' Tran said. 'As you shall soon see. Shall we go in?'

'After you, Colonel Tran.

They stepped inside and surveyed the interior. There were only three people inside the long narrow little saloon. All Europeans, they seemed bored, appearing to have been washed up and hung out to dry in the tough game of life. Their listless eyes reflected faded dreams and staggering disappointments. These were failed white men clinging together in the midst of a yellow society.

A row of small tables, each only capable of accommodating two or three people, lined one wall while a scarred bar took over most of the remainder of the room. A bartender, quite Teutonic and very tough looking, glanced their way. '*Oui, messieurs?*' He invited them to sit down by indicating a couple of stools in front of him.

'*Nous desirons parler avec vous*, Hosteins,' Tran said motioning the man to follow them toward the back of the place.

'*Sheist!*' Hosteins cursed. But he followed them.

Andrews glanced at the wall and noted two certificates hung out in plain sight. The first sported an illustration of the French army parachutist badge and proclaimed:

REPUBLIQUE FRANCAISE
MINISTERE DES ARMEES
BREVET MILITAIRE
DE
PARACHUTISTE
a
Légionnaire 2e Classe HOSTEINS, Bruno

The second, showing various insignia and a blue, white and red ribbon bore printing which said:

Sergent HOSTEINS, Bruno
2e BATAILLON ETRANGER DE PARACHUTISTES
EVADE DE DIEN BIEN PHU

The trio went into the tiny office at the far end of the bar. Tran pushed the door open and motioned the bartender to precede them. After Andrews had crowded in, the door was shut and the Vietnamese pointed to the only chair. 'Sit down.' He indicated the American with a nod of his head. 'This is Mister Andrews –' His head bobbed the other way. '– This is Hosteins.'

Hosteins shrugged. 'What do you want?'

'Mister Andrews wants to talk to you,' Tran said.

'Make it snappy,' Hosteins said. 'I've business to attend to.'

'He'll take as much time as he wishes,' Tran said.

Andrews made himself comfortable on the desk beside Hosteins. 'I hear you are familiar with a place called Fort Rollet.'

'Yes,' Hosteins said.

'I understand you know every inch of it.'

'I helped build it,' Hosteins said. 'What is this all about?'

'And I also understand you are very familiar with the area around it,' Andrews continued.

'I have probably walked – or crawled – every bit of two hundred square kilometers around Fort Rollet,' Hosteins said, 'What do you want to know about it?'

'Would you like to see it again?'

Hosteins displayed a slight smile. 'Not particularly. It is up in the north – between Lai Chiau and Dien Bien Phu.' Did you notice my certificates on the wall?'

'Yes, if my French doesn't fail me, it identifies you as an escapee of Dien Bien Phu,' Andrews said.

'Correct, *monsieur*,' Hosteins said. 'But that doesn't actually tell the full story. I was a *successful* escapee – there were many, many *attempted* escapees. *Mais, c'est mauvais*, there was no certificate issued for that. And having gone to all the trouble of avoiding capture up there some ten years ago, I have no desire to repeat the risk.'

'It can be made worth your while,' Andrews said.

'Sorry, but –'

'Bah!' Tran snorted. 'Enough of this prattle! Hosteins, you are coming with us and accepting assignment on a special mission. And there is absolutely no chance for you to get out of it.'

Hosteins snarled. 'You have no right –'

Andrews spoke in a cold voice. 'Bruno Hosteins, ex-sergeant, French Foreign Legion. Enlisted in 1946 and served until the honorable expiration of your second enlistment contract in 1956.'

'Yes,' Hosteins said. 'And by virtue of that service I am a citizen of France and a legal resident of South Vietnam. All my papers are in first class order.'

Andrews continued. 'Horst Kruger, *SS-obersturmfuhrer, 3rd SS Panzer Division – Totenkopf.*'

Hosteins shrugged. 'So? That is no big secret. When I enlisted in the Foreign Legion from the POW cage in Stuttgart, I was in the full uniform of the *Waffen-SS*. The Legion offered a new life and a new name. That is standard procedure. I am no war criminal. I served in a front line combat unit.'

'Absolutely correct,' Andrews said. 'And nobody in the west has any charges against you whatsoever. But how would you like to see East Germany? They would love to get their hands on any ex-SS man – particularly one who had a long record of fighting various Communist causes. And they're not real particular about making bonafide charges. The Reds are quite good at making things up.'

'You have no right to send me there,' Hosteins said. 'I am a legal French citizen!'

Andrews' friendly countenance faded, and his expression hardened. 'I don't give a goddamn if you're the president of France, Hosteins. If I want to slap your ass right down in the middle of East Germany – or the Soviet Union – I'll do it.'

Hosteins grimaced. 'I will appeal to the French embassy.'

'There will be no opportunity for that,' Tran said coldly.

'On the other hand,' Andrews said now smiling, 'what would you think of going to America – with lots of cash?'

'I have a brother –'

'In New Jersey,' Andrews interrupted. 'Rural Route 7 outside of the little town of Sand Brook. Karl Kruger wasn't in the SS, was he? In fact, he's quite a bit younger than you, Hosteins. He didn't serve in World War II at all. After that unpleasant occurrence ended, he emigrated to America. He ran a little camera shop in Paterson, New Jersey. After a couple of years he sold out and bought a farm. From what I've been able to find out, he's really enjoying life to the hilt. And, guess what? He's got room – and work – for you there.'

Hosteins betrayed his emotions. 'He's asked me to come

there. But I've not been able to get a visa. And it's a nice farm. Karl wrote me about it. He has big plans, and with the little money I've put aside I could –'

'What about a visa *and* several thousand dollars to go along with your savings, Hosteins?' Andrews asked. 'You two could really enlarge the operation, huh? And I'll bet those three kids of his would love to meet their uncle Bruno – or – Horst. He has a lovely wife too. Sounds ideal to me.'

'How much will you pay me?'

Tran interrupted. 'Don't speak as if you're bargaining, Hosteins. I haven't time to listen to this mindless prattle. If you're going to America you'd better make arrangements to sell this place.'

'I still need that visa from the American Embassy,' Hosteins said. 'It takes time.'

'Your visa is ready and waiting for you when you return from the mission,' Andrews said.

Tran's patience had at last run out. 'Where do you want him to report?'

'We have a safehouse, but I can't give the address, of course,' Andrews said. 'I'll personally pick you up here in four hours.'

Hosteins was angry. 'I cannot possibly sell my business in that short time.'

Andrews smiled. 'We'll get to that, Hosteins. How much do you want for it?'

Doctor Yoon Hwan and Colonel Nguyen Chi Roi stood by the flagpole in the middle of the prison yard and watched Lieutenant Colonel Winston Baldwin, still naked, walk toward them. The guard behind the prisoner prodded him every few steps. They finally stopped.

The guard barked the order. 'Salute flag!'

Baldwin hesitated, then remembered the sergeant's advice. STAY HEALTHY. Even if they weren't keeping him in that box, he was still receiving an inadequate diet. And the trips out into the hot sun were beginning to turn his skin a bright pink. A bad sunburn could lead to serious infection for an undernourished man.

'Salute flag!'

Any type of infection would lead to a fever. And a fever under those unsanitary conditions would inevitably be an extremely high one. The type that would lead to delirium – and men babble things when they're sunk that low. Things they might not want other people to know.

'Salute flàg!'

Baldwin hesitated a moment, then slowly raised his hand to his brow – and held it.

'Excellent, Colonel Baldwin!' Yoon said. He turned to Nguyen. 'What do you think of that, comrade?'

Nguyen snarled. 'I think he has a long way to go before I am satisfied with him. And that includes answering our questions.'

Yoon laughed in good humor. 'Oh, my dear Colonel Nguyen. I'm sure that my friend here is more than ready to open up his heart to us and aid the great socialist cause by making us fully informed of all the useful information he has.'

'I want something to eat,' Baldwin said.

'You have already been fed!' Nguyen barked.

'That was two days ago,' Baldwin said. 'I want something to eat.'

'You talk with Doctor Yoon first,' Nguyen said. 'Then we'll see if – and what – you are to eat.'

'Yes! Yes!' Yoon said. 'Please, come with me to my quarters Colonel Baldwin. We will have a nice chat.'

'Not until I have a chance to bathe and get some clothes,' Baldwin said. He had purposely asked for this after requesting food. He understood a little how the Oriental mind worked. To demand only one thing would make them appear to lose face if they gave in to it. However, if he requested three items, they would still appear to have the upper hand by granting him only two.

Nguyen gave quick orders, and the guard trotted away toward a nearby building. Within moments he was back with a small bundle of clothing. He flung them to the ground at Baldwin's feet. The American bent down and picked them up. The guard motioned him to a spot across the compound where a small outdoor shower stood. The prospect of cleaning up added haste to Baldwin's pace as they walked across the prison compound.

The water, from a well, was cold and refreshing. There was no soap, so the prisoner contented himself with rubbing himself clean with his hands. Then, still soaking wet because of no towel, he turned his attention to the items of clothing. They were prison garb of a sort, trousers and jacket, with white and red stripes. He slipped into the pants. They were too large.

'I need a smaller size.'

Nguyen frowned at this impertinence. 'That's the only size. Do you think we run a tailor shop for imperialist criminals?'

Baldwin was insistent. He indicated the trousers wouldn't stay up. 'Then may I have a belt?'

'You have jacket, pants and cloth sandals. That is all!' Nguyen yelled at him.

Yoon placed a kindly hand on Baldwin's shoulder. 'Please, Colonel. Be grateful.' He motioned toward the North Vietnamese officer. 'Thank him for these gifts from the people.'

Baldwin's face blanched with anger – but the sergeant's advice leaped once again into his mind. STAY HEALTHY. He gave a cursory glance toward Nguyen. 'Thanks.'

'Oh, no, my dear Colonel Baldwin,' Yoon said. 'You must thank him properly. And bow to him.'

Baldwin hesitated, then damned his personal feelings. He bowed. 'Thank you for the clothing.'

'And how did you get the clothing?' Yoon asked.

'They were given to me,' Baldwin said puzzled.

'You received them through the kindness and benevolence of the people of North Vietnam,' Yoon said. 'Now you must tell Colonel Nguyen that.'

Baldwin took a deep breath. 'Thank you for this clothing – I've received through the kindness of the North Vietnamese people.'

Again Yoon displayed his friendly smile. 'Now, was that really that difficult, Colonel? And saluting the flag was quite easy too.'

I'll soon reach the point where I'll have to draw the line, Baldwin's mind told him. *Or these sons of bitches will have me dancing on the end of a string before another week is out.*

'You have gotten away with too much,' Nguyen said to Baldwin. 'I have not punished you with the severity you deserve out of my respect for Doctor Yoon. His kindness toward you is misplaced, and you are taking advantage of him.'

'Not at all! Not at all!' Yoon said pleasantly. 'Well, come, Colonel Baldwin. Let us go over to my quarters for a nice chat.'

The two walked toward the front gate. Doctor Yoon lived in a newly constructed frame dwelling situated between the tall cement wall that formed the principal barrier of the prison, and the barbed wire fence which formed the secondary containment feature of the installation.

They were let through the gate and during the short stroll to the doctor's residence, Baldwin's eyes swept the area with all the expertise of a trained fighter pilot. He took in the layout of the land, each guard post, the towers, number of strands of barbed wire and the small garrison outside the compound. He turned and looked back toward the main prison. This was his first time to see it. His initial entrance had been done when blindfolded.

They stopped at the doctor's door and the Korean opened it. 'Please go in, Colonel.'

'Thank you.' Baldwin instantly regretted the words of gratitude. He had to reach a happy medium of not antagonizing them, yet not letting them – or more importantly, himself – start thinking he appreciated the small favors or courtesies shown him.

The interior of the bungalow was simple and quite oriental. A wood cookstove stood off to one side, and a narrow bed had been situated near a window. There were some shelves for cookware, plates and a few personal items. A plain wooden table and matching chairs, completed the room's decor.

'Would you like some tea, Colonel?' Yoon asked.

'No, thank you.'

'Please, don't feel you're belittling yourself by accepting my hospitality,' Yoon said. 'After all, Colonel Nguyen isn't here to observe us.' He waited a moment for Baldwin to accept, and when he didn't, the Korean said, 'I'll fix you some anyway. I'm sure you'll enjoy a cup.'

Baldwin eased toward the window to see the part of the outer fence that had been blocked from his vision during the walk to the cottage.

'I'm afraid I have no snacks here,' Yoon said putting the water on to boil. 'We eat in the messhall and, of course, there are no stores nearby.' He seemed to hesitate. 'But I suppose I could get a few things – if you'd like.'

'No, thank you,' Baldwin said. Even though the extra food

would give him needed strength, he felt this wasn't the time to try for it.

'Please, sit down,' Yoon said. 'Make yourself comfortable.'

Baldwin, who had felt ridiculous standing there holding onto the trousers to keep them from falling to his ankles, took a chair. He remained silent, listening to Yoon's small talk until his host came to the table with the tea. It smelled delicious, and there was sugar, lemon and cream on the tray too. He felt if he had only a cup –

Doped! The goddamned stuff was probably doped!

'I don't care for any,' he said tersely.

'Oh, I am sorry,' Yoon said. He poured himself a cup and put in all the condiments available. He took several deep drinks and smiled at Baldwin, seeming to read his thoughts. 'See? It isn't drugged.'

'I don't care for any,' Baldwin repeated.

'Well . . . if you change your mind,' Yoon said. 'I do hope these little visits we have prove beneficial, Colonel Baldwin.'

'We're going to have more?'

'Of course. But you'll be talking with Colonel Nguyen too,' Yoon said. Then he lowered his voice. 'I'm afraid these Vietnamese are such . . . well, barbarians!' He shuddered. 'They have a long way to go before they're ready for the civilized socialist order. But, during times of struggle, even the savage can be useful now and then.'

'I wouldn't know,' Baldwin said. He knew Yoon's derogatory remarks about the Communist Vietnamese were designed to produce a mood of intimacy and agreement between them. 'My own people came out of that a few thousand years ago.'

Yoon smiled. 'Really? How interesting. And I must admit a sincere admiration for western technology. For example, your airplane. Would you care to tell me a bit about it?'

The question was put so crudely that Baldwin knew Yoon didn't expect an answer. 'All I'm going to give is my name, rank and service number.'

'Of course.' Yoon finished his tea. 'Sure you don't care for a cup?'

'Positive.'

'In that case, I shall allow you to return to your cell.' Yoon got up and went to the door and opened it. A guard stepped in and motioned to Baldwin. Yoon nodded to him on the way out. 'I shall look forward to our next visit – and I'm sure you will too.'

The walk back took but a few minutes. When they reached the cell block, Colonel Nguyen was waiting for him. The North Vietnamese sneered openly. 'Enjoy your tea?'

Baldwin said nothing.

Nguyen pulled a device from his pocket. It was a block of wood with a number 5 painted on it. A piece of twine had been strung through a hole drilled through it. Nguyen put it around Baldwin's neck. 'From now on you have no name. You are Number Five, understood?'

'Yes.'

'That is how you will be referred to from this moment on.' He spoke to the guard and the cell door was opened. 'Inside, Number Five!' He kicked Baldwin hard in the buttocks knocking him into the cell and across the bunk. 'Tomorrow you will visit with me and enjoy *my* hospitality, Number Five.'

Baldwin sat up on the bunk and watched the door slam shut. After a few moments there was some scraping and tapping on the wall. It was the sergeant named Dayton tapping out another message:

S-H-I-T – H-A-S – H-I-T – F-A-N

THREE

'You are one no good sonofabitch, Andy. You know that?' Captain Robert Falconi tossed the dossier back on the desk that sat between himself and Clayton Andrews.

'Am I really that bad?'

'You sure as hell are,' Falconi said. 'This poor bastard Hosteins first started fighting commies back in 1941. And that was right in the heartland of good ol' Mother Russia itself. Then he did it again in Indo-China from 1946 until 1954. And if that wasn't enough, he scrapped with 'em again in Algeria from '54 to '56. Then, finally, after ten years in the goddamned French Foreign Legion he gets out and comes back to the one place he learned to love – Saigon. Not to run a black market or whores or dope or anything illegal. All he wanted to do was own a bar – a little ol' bar that doesn't make much money, but provides him with a small living and a chance to deal with the types of people he prefers. And you fuck that up – asshole that you are.'

Andrews nodded. 'Right.'

'You put the squeeze on the guy telling him that if he don't play ball with you, you're gonna snatch him and drop him right in the middle of East Germany or the Soviet Union.'

'Don't forget I could run his ass up north too,' Andrews reminded him.

'Oh, yeah. I'm sure you covered all options in throwing a royal fucking into the guy,' Falconi said.

'But I'm also seeing to it that he's going to be well paid and – get this – being granted a permanent resident alien visa for the good ol' U.S. of A.'

Falconi smirked. 'Yeah. If he don't get zapped first.'

'Yeah, well, he might,' Andrews conceded. 'But after you get the briefing on this next mission, you're gonna be happy as hell to have ex-legionnaire Hosteins along for the ride.'

'We'll see about that,' Falconi said seriously. 'Frankly, I don't like fucking over this guy.'

'He's ex-*Waffen SS* for Chrissake!' Andrews exclaimed. 'That should make the Jewish part of your blood boil.'

'Well, it don't,' Falconi said. 'In my world it's the commies that are the bad guys. As far as I know there isn't even a viable Nazi threat around for me to concentrate on. When there is, I'll take it on.'

'Believe me, Falcon,' Andrews said using the other's nickname. 'I wouldn't have gone to all the trouble of recruiting Hosteins unless he was a real asset – and he is.'

'Then there's no sense in us arguing until I get the full picture,' Falconi said. The captain was a big man, six feet, one inch tall and powerfully built with a wide chest, broad shoulders and long strong limbs. His jet black hair was cut short, and his gaze from his sea green eyes was intense and aggressive. The man was the professional soldier personified.

Captain Falconi was the commanding officer of a unique outfit called the Black Eagles. This special combat team was comprised of the best jungle fighters in the United States – from all services: be it the army's multi-skilled Special Forces, the navy's deadly SEALS, the marine corps' tough recon teams, or even the more sophisticated specialists of the air force.

A part of the clandestine SOG – Special Operations Group – in Southeast Asia, the Black Eagles drew the dirtiest, deadliest and most dangerous assignments in an escalating war that was to prove to be the most brutal in American history.

The outfit, like many others in Southeast Asia, wore a self-designed, locally produced insignia that was unauthorized as far as regulations went. They sported a blue sleeve patch in the shape of an arrow-head. In the center of the device was a black eagle holding a red lightning bolt in one claw and a gold sword in the other.

Falconi settled back in his chair. 'Let's knock off the bullshit, I'm ready for my preliminary briefing.'

'Okay. Here goes.' Andrews stood up and went to a wall map showing both North and South Vietnam. He took a pointer and laid the tip of it at a place close to the Chinese border. 'Here at almost the exact midpoint between Lai Chiau and Dien Bien Phu is a place the bad guys have dubbed Garrison Three.'

'One of their army posts?' Falconi asked.

'No. It's a very special prison camp run by their top warden, a mean character named Colonel Nguyen Chi Roi. And if it wasn't bad enough that he's in charge, there's a real pisser from North Korea there advising him. And he's an old hand at tormenting American prisoners, having served his apprenticeship during the Korean War on American pilots. His name is Doctor Yoon Hwan.'

'What kind of doctor?' Falconi wanted to know.

'Ph.D in human behaviour, University of Moscow and the KGB Academy,' Andrews said. 'He's written a couple of books – and he's good at what he does.'

'Brainwashing?'

'Exactly,' Andrews answered. 'And the little son of a bitch is so subtle, his subjects hardly know what's going on. He works in conjunction with others, and he simply manifests their efforts through very friendly persuasion.'

'And he's good, huh?'

'If he had enough time he could probably convince you that having your sister commit fallatio on the horses of a Mongolian cavalry squadron would somehow enhance her life.'

'I don't have a sister.'

'Don't be a wiseass, Falconi!' Andrews said.

'Can't help it,' Falconi said with a grin. 'Okay, so far I know there's a prison up north called Garrison Three that is being run by the two best experts in the Communist Far East. Are the Black Eagles supposed to snatch them?'

'Right,' Andrews answered. 'Along with getting the prisoners they hold the hell out of there.'

Falconi frowned. 'You mean I have to traipse through the jungle with a trainload of prisoners?'

'There's only five being held there,' Andrews said.

Falconi whistled. 'Jesus! The place has got to be very special – then the people held there must be VIPs, right?'

Andrews went back to his drawer and pulled out a list. He handed it over to Falconi. 'Read for yourself.'

> BALDWIN, Winston R., Lieutenant Colonel, United States Air Force. Detached from regular duties and assigned TDY to Special Reconnaissance Squadron, MACV/SOG, as operations officer. Shot down June 1964.

DAYTON, Marvin G., Staff Sergeant, United States Army, military advisor attached to various ARVN units as part of a special evaluation team. Captured during operations to locate an enemy radio station near the village of Ap Bac in the Plain of Reeds in January 1963.

LAM, Phu, Brigadier General, ARVN, G-2 for IV Corps. Kidnapped off the streets of Saigon while on leave in September 1963.

CHIN, Lau, Vietnamese born ethnic Chinese. CIA agent and saboteur. Arrested in Hanoi in March 1964.

TRINH, Duc, Colonel, NVA. Deputy director of Viet Cong operations. Attempted to defect through aid of Chin Lau. Arrested in Hanoi in March 1964.

'I can't overemphasize the importance of getting Baldwin out of there,' Andrews said. 'The man should never have been allowed to fly a mission.'

Falconi put the list back on the desk. 'Liberating these people may be a real problem, even if there are only five of 'em. Do you know their physical conditions? After those two torture experts have been wringing them out, the poor bastards may be in no shape to take a jungle hike.'

'Right,' Andrews answered. 'There's going to be a doctor and a highly trained medical corpsman – both from the navy – going along with you.'

'Then where does this poor bastard Hosteins come in?' Falconi asked.

'The place dubbed the Garrison Three was a former French Foreign Legion post called Fort Rollet. Legionnaires built it, and built it well. Plumbing, electricity, the whole nine yards. Hosteins was a platoon leader there. He supervised most of the work and knows the place like his own bathroom. He also not only took part in operations in the vicinity of the post, but when Dien Bien Phu fell, he wandered around from one end of that area to the other evading capture.'

'Interesting,' Falconi mused.

Andrews grinned. 'Now what do you think of me putting the arm on the guy?'

Falconi smiled back. 'Andy, sometimes you're so goddamned smart, you boggle the mind.' He paused and lit a cigarette.

'Okay. Now that I know what the mission is, let's hear the execution.'

'Simple and fast,' Andrews said. 'You'll go in via parachute from an Air America C-130.'

'HALO?' Falconi asked.

'Nope. No High Altitude Low Openings this trip. Strictly conventional T10 stuff. The area is sparsely populated. You'll be winging in over from the Laotian border and unassing on a DZ not all that far from your objective. That DZ becomes an LZ on the way out. You'll call in choppers for exfiltration.'

'More Air America?'

'Right.'

'It looks like there's going to be quite a bit of walking involved there – over hill and dale through thick jungle,' Falconi remarked.

'Indeed,' Andrews said. 'And it's going to be slow moving through thick jungle. You'll have to avoid trails.'

'Then there's one guy I'm going to insist goes along on this,' Falconi said.

Andrews nodded. 'I figured that out. Dobbs, right?'

'That's my boy.'

'Sorry,' Andrews said. 'I tried to pull him out of that MI Detachment of his, but he'd punched out the first sergeant and gone AWOL a couple of weeks back.'

'That stupid sonofabitch!' Falconi blurted. 'He's the best fucking tracker and point man in the U.S. Army. You could throw him into a vat of black ink and tell him to emerge on azimuth 203 and he'd do it – not 202 or 204, but 203!'

'Have any idea where you might locate him?' Andrews asked. 'And we haven't got a whole lot of time. When you get the full blown briefing, you'll see what I mean.'

'I know exactly where to find that crazy bastard,' Falconi said. 'And the first thing I'm gonna do when I leave here is dig him out.'

'Hope you can locate the guy,' Andrews said. 'I want to see him go along too.'

'By the way,' Falconi said. 'What if some of those prisoners have been wrung out so bad there's no sense in trying to liberate 'em?'

Again Andrews reached in his desk drawer. He tossed a small, brown packet over to Falconi. 'That's what these are for.'

'Big jolt of a stimulant?' Falconi asked.

'I don't think cyanide is classified as a stimulant,' Andrews said dryly.

'Why not let the medics administer a large overdose of morphine?' Falconi asked.

'You know the deal on that,' Andrews said. 'We always keep such activities quiet even where personnel with proper clearance are concerned. It's always a touchy situation and the smaller number of people involved, the better. Besides, in the light of possibly snuffing a USAF officer, it might be bad for the medic's morale.'

'Hell, it's not exactly a big boost for my own morale either,' Falconi said sourly.

'Number Five! Number Five!' The guard's voice grated into Baldwin's sleep.

He opened his eyes and tried to figure out what was going on.

'Number Five! Number Five!'

There was a sudden rapping on his cell door and Baldwin could hear the key in the padlock. Then he remembered. *He* was Number Five.

'On your feet! Outside Number Five! Outside Number Five!'

Baldwin shuffled through the door and into the pale yellow glare of the large flashlight. He was immediately struck from the side so hard it staggered him.

'You get tag! You get tag!'

Baldwin remembered the wooden number he was supposed to wear around his neck. He went back to his cell and emerged with it in place. There were two guards, he realized now, and each grabbed an arm and frog-marched him across the compound to the fence. When they arrived he saw a cage had been built in the wire.

'You go! You go! Through people's gate!' the guard yelped pointing at the opening.

Baldwin saw he would have to get down on his hands and knees and crawl through the thing. Another glance in the light revealed two more guards waiting for him on the other side. A vicious kick into the back of his thigh sent him moving, and he dropped down and went through the deep, stinking mud on all fours. When he arrived on the other side, the warders pushed him into the muck and grabbed his arms, shackling them behind his back. Then they dragged him to his feet and, in doing so, caused the overly-large trousers to come off and stay in the mud. The cloth sandals he had gotten that afternoon were also left back in the goo.

Again he was rushed, this time up to a small cement building in a cluster of similar edifices located in the center of the compound. One of the guards knocked on the door and pushed it open. Then they hurtled Baldwin through so hard he lost his balance and crashed to the floor. With his hands cuffed behind his back, he was unable to break the fall. All he could do was turn his face to avoid striking it.

Colonel Nguyen, sitting behind a table, bellowed in rage and rushed around to kick him hard. 'On your feeet, Number Five! You don't relax in the presence of the commandant!'

Baldwin struggled to regain his balance and finally managed to do so, but not before sustaining several hard bruising kicks that left his buttocks and ribs sore as boils.

'You stand at attention in front of the commandant!' Nguyen ordered in an angry voice.

Baldwin assumed the position of attention. This was a new twist to the game. The colonel had never played the role of the commandant before. The prisoner stood there while Nguyen meticulously went over the papers on the table. He worked slowly, initialing each document in its turn before going to the next.

Baldwin wasn't sure how much time had passed, he had sunk into his own mental stupor, his mind wandering from disjointed thought to disjointed thought. Suddenly he realized he'd fallen to the floor.

'Get up, Number Five! Get up! Get up!' Nguyen again hurried around the table to deliver kicks and blows until Baldwin managed to regain his feet. 'You stand at attention! Don't move!' The NVA officer slapped his prisoner's face. 'And keep your eyes open!'

Baldwin fought it, but too many days without adequate food and rest had taken its grim toll. The longer he stood, the more his knees ached. It was a deep pain in the joints, not like anything he had ever felt before. He fought it and gritted his teeth against it, until, finally a moan escaped his lips.

'Shut up, Number Five!' Nguyen shrieked in rage. This time he leaped across the table and drove his fist straight into Baldwin's stomach. 'Shut up! Shut up! Shut up! Shut up!'

Baldwin gasped and went down. More kicks and he tried to scramble to an erect position, but, with his hands behind his back, his balance was gone in a dizzy swirl until he rolled across the floor in a desperate attempt to escape Nguyen's heavy kicks.

The colonel finally stopped and allowed Baldwin to get to his feet. 'You cannot stand, Number Five? Then we shall help you!' He went to the door and yelled out some words in his own language. Two guards immediately appeared with a rope. They grabbed Baldwin and pulled him to a position in the center of the room. They unshackled his wrists and tied them together as tightly as they could, then tossed the rope over a rafter just above him. The soldiers pulled it tight, hauling Baldwin's arms above his head to a point where only the tips of his toes touched the floor.

Nguyen laughed aloud. 'Do you know how ridiculous you look, Number Five! Wearing a baggy striped jacket, no shoes or pants with your muddy penis and ass showing as plain as your big Anglo-Saxon nose?'

Baldwin said nothing, but gritted his teeth against the pain of the grinding in his shoulder joints.

Nguyen walked up to him and drove his knee up into the American's scrotum. Baldwin gasped in agony, then gagged as his empty stomach reacted with dry heaves to the mistreatment. His throat felt like it had been wiped out with sandpaper and his crotch blazed with pain.

The North Vietnamese giggled at his helpless prisoner. 'And to think I've only started with you.'

FOUR

Captain Robert Falconi pulled the Chevrolet sedan to the curb and stepped out. He was dressed as a civilian, wearing a short-sleeved, loose flowing shirt, slacks and loafers. The officer was immediately besieged by a mob of screeching urchins. He picked out the biggest and toughest looking kid, tossed him a few coins to keep an eye on the car, then stepped back in the street to survey the buildings before him.

This was Yen Do Street in the Cholon district of Saigon. Here the blackmarketeers, pimps, whores, dope dealers and other criminals ruled the roost. And here also, Falconi knew well, was where SGT Archie Dobbs would be holed up. A sign above the store notified the passing public that there were rooms for rent upstairs.

Falconi walked past the grocery to an opening that led to an alley. He stepped through and started for a flight of rickety stairs when the sight of three hardcore bodyguard types stopped him. A big illegal deal of one kind or another was going down, no doubt, and these hoods were the security. Somewhere in the vicinity, thousands of dollars was passing from one pair of hands to another to finalize the transaction.

Naturally the folks involved would be in a nervous and apprehensive mood – especially with an American suddenly showing up. This put Falconi in a bad spot – if he continued, the trio of Oriental toughs would attack to keep him from crashing in on the deal. And if he tried a hasty retreat, they would figure he was off to bring in more heat. Falconi shrugged to himself. *Well, I'm fucked if I do and fucked if I don't. What the hell, having Archie Dobbs along on the mission is worth it.*

He tensed and moved forward.

They came at him in an arrow formation, the tip of their 'missile' a big Chinese with a murderous face that must have made his mother shudder. His aggressive movements advertised that there would be a complete lack of social preliminaries to the encounter.

Falconi blocked an overhead karate chop with his left forearm and stabbed the tips of his stiffened fingers into the soft spot between the man's adam's apple and chin. The first attacker staggered backward, hands clutching his throat, eyes expanded in amazement and pain. He wilted to the ground as his partner closed in from Falconi's left and slashed a tiger-claw stroke at the American's face.

Instantly Falconi pivoted and drove a snap kick that bit deep into the exposed armpit of the second attacker. A scream of pain, as sincere as it was loud, announced the success of the American's technique. The man stood quivering, stunned by the kick to the nerve cluster under his arm. Falconi slashed a fist to the side of the aggressor's jaw and the man joined his comrade in the dirt.

The third man, more prudent and perhaps more dangerous as well, displayed a talent for patience his friends didn't have. He stepped back a half dozen paces and assumed the *ding bo* position, which is disarming in that it portrays casual relaxation even though the entire body is coiled for instantaneous reaction to the slightest sign of unfriendliness from a potential opponent.

Falconi sensed the fellow's talent.

The American circled slowly to the right, trying to edge the Oriental into an area stacked with boxes. Falconi figured that would hinder his movements somewhat. The man solved the problem by kicking apart two of the crates in as many explosive kicks that took him all of one second flat.

Falconi was impressed.

The man who suffered the indignity to his armpit had recovered sufficiently to rejoin the fray. Although one arm was useless, he had another as well as his two feet still in operational order. And he was angry – not like a street punk – but with the calculating ire of a highly trained martial artist. He wouldn't be losing his head and making any more rash moves.

Falconi feinted toward the healthy one, then took the expected charge of the other. The heel of his hand didn't connect with the point of the guy's chin like he wanted. But he did hit him along the jawline hard enough to stun him. Falconi improvised quickly by grabbing his opponent and displaying a fine exhibition of a shoulder throw – at the other with his buddy.

But the guy came in under his flying comrade and delivered a straight stamp kick at Falconi. It connected enough to send the American somersaulting backward. He was on his feet in time to throw out two quick ramhead punches that missed. But they made the guy draw off, unable to complete the attack.

Now the other man, still with a bad arm and a worse disposition, had showed he was still game and wanted to play some more. He joined his friend and they drew apart. Now it was Falconi being forced into a corner. He decided to stop conscious thought and let his *ki* direct his actions. The hours and hours of meditation had brought about an uplifting of his subconscious that permitted a near instinctive use of fighting skills acquired over years of steady, unrelenting practice.

The assault came.

Falconi went low to avoid a slashing knife-hand stroke, then came up with a quick spinning-wheel kick. The back of his heel crushed into the side of the closest opponent's head with the force of a rifle butt-stroke. The guy went down and stayed down. A concussion and dislocated neck can be a hell of a sedative.

The last attacker was startled by the American's move. He backed away quickly, but his hands were still poised for battle. Falconi feinted a snap kick for the man's groin. The thug's hands moved to guard his privates, leaving his face and head exposed. Falconi's other leg swung a fast roundhouse kick to the guy's temple. The Oriental did an awkward sideways shuffle into a wall, and slumped to the ground unconscious with a fractured skull.

Falconi breathed a long sigh of relief. It had been that or nothing. One miss and it would have been all she wrote.

'Nice move, Falconi,' came an American voice from above. 'I didn't think you was gonna pull it off.'

Falconi snarled. 'Archie, you bastard!' He spun and glanced up to see the sergeant standing in an open window.

Dobbs displayed the .45 in his hand. 'I wouldn't have let 'em finish you.'

'Get your ass down here, Dobbs, *now!*'

'You bet, Skipper,' Dobbs said grinning. 'You know what I always say. "You call, I haul, that's all!" '

* * *

Colonel Nguyen Chi Roi strolled from the headquarters building across the bare no man's land between the prison wall and barbed wire fence to Doctor Yoon's quarters. He knocked politely and waited to be invited to enter.

The doctor, finishing up a mid-day repast of rice and freshly caught fish, invited his colleague to join him.

'No, thank you, Doctor,' Nguyen said. 'I eat but twice a day. A hearty breakfast and then a very light supper late at night.'

Yoon pushed his plates aside. 'Has Baldwin been returned to his cell?'

'Yes. We left him hanging until almost noon. He was still unconscious when we left him on his bunk.'

Yoon nodded. 'Any serious injuries from the treatment?'

'His left shoulder is out of place,' Nguyen answered. 'Not critical but very painful.'

'And you left it that way?'

'Yes, of course,' Nguyen said.

'Good. I think it best he not see me for about three days or so. Some rough physical treatment should soften him up,' Yoon said.

'When should we begin the questioning?'

'Not until the day before I meet with him. I always found it best to keep up a steady program of pain that seems almost without reason. Then a few questions that should be relatively easy for him to answer. Ease off, then repeat the process. Pain – questions – pain – questions, until the prisoner's subconscious connects the answering of questions with the lessening of pain.'

Nguyen shook his head. 'It doesn't seem it will work. Particularly on a man like Baldwin. He's well educated, patriotic and highly intelligent.'

Yoon smiled. 'That, comrade, is why we must break down his mental processes while at the same time feed his brain the reactions we want from it. The real application to that part of our program begins with the phase in which we deny him sleep. I learned these things well working with other Americans, who were also pilots, during my country's war with the Americans.'

'We must perfect our own skills as quickly as possible,' Nguyen said. 'Our continued operations in the south will soon goad the Americans into action – as it is designed to do – and if they begin a concentrated program of aerial attacks on North

Vietnam we will soon have many prisoners. At that time speed will be most important in getting vital intelligence out of them.'

Yoon chuckled. 'Speed? You have no need for speed in thc long run, comrade. You Vietnamese may sit back and prolong this war as long as you like. Time is on your side, and the Americans will never fully commit themselves to Southeast Asia. They'll want to make a token effort of sorts, pay a bloody price then sit down and negotiate. This will eventually be an unpopular war in America. Our efforts in the struggle will be helped along with pressure from both America's leftists and the public at large. And, once more, you may utilize time – that so precious commodity that must be used wisely.'

'As a soldier, I display too much impatience, comrade,' Nguyen said. 'I thank you for enlightening me with your wise counsel.'

Yoon smiled. 'I am here to help, comrade.' He paused. 'What is the status of the other four prisoners.'

'The traitor Trinh is near death.'

'His condition has not improved?' Yoon asked with concern.

'I'm sorry. No.'

'Then I suggest we get him to a proper hospital as soon as possible,' Yoon said. 'He must be in shape to stand trial.'

'Of course, comrade. Chin is giving every indication of complete insanity. Your work in that area was most remarkable,' Nguyen said. 'I did not think he would break.'

Yoon smiled. 'Physical pain, even when skilfully applied, is only part of a concentrated plan, Comrade Colonel. Without its being carefully combined with applied mental anguish, it is useful only as a punishment. Again, sleeplessness was the main catalyst of our efforts.'

'Lam is certainly responding well in that phase,' Nguyen said continuing his report. 'He has been kept awake now for ninety hours. He is close to being completely incoherent.'

'Good. He will have much useful information for us,' Yoon said. 'And the American sergeant?'

'He has almost recovered completely,' Nguyen said. 'I was surprised that you wanted to keep him. Any tactical information he might have is now hopelessly out of date.'

'Propaganda value, my dear Colonel,' Yoon said. 'His unit, the Special Forces, is getting too popular with the American people. Particularly in light of the late President Kennedy giving them permission to wear their green berets after that sordid headgear had been taken away. We must drum up some detrimental propaganda against them. And when we parade Sergeant Dayton before the cameras, we want him to appear bright and alert, yet obviously defeated and sincerely apologetic.' Then the North Korean became thoughtful. 'But there is something about that man that puzzles me – an intangible quality that makes me think he has a motive for everything he does, and for every statement he makes, and for the way in which he answers each and every question put to him.'

Nguyen shrugged. 'He was most stubborn and evasive during questioning, I admit, but he has performed well in other areas. He reads the books and pamphlets we supply him and listens carefully when the visiting commissar lectures him. He responds well when asked to comment on what we've taught him.'

'Yet there is an enigma about the man,' Yoon said with a worried expression. 'He is either giving us full cooperation, or playing what the Americans call a "con game".'

Master Sergeant John Snow, operations/team sergeant of the Black Eagles stood tall and severe, the clipboard tucked under one brawny arm while he watched the arriving men climb off the back of the deuce-and-a-half truck in front of the isolation centre at Tan Son Nhut Air Base.

The area, set aside for SOG's special airborne operations, was well guarded and out of the way of other installations on the sprawling complex. An ARVN infantry unit, made up of purely defensive weapons, including heavy machine guns and mortars, surrounded the place. It wasn't expected they could hold off a determined numerically superior attack for any great length of time – just long enough so that any classified documents or material inside could be destroyed.

Another truck rolled up, and MSG Snow checked off the names of the men as they arrived, until his roster was complete. The last vehicle to arrive was a civilian sedan. The back door opened and two men came out. One, Falconi, wore slightly soiled civilian clothing as if he'd been in a fight. The other, a short husky man with his skull nearly shaven wore only a pair of fatigue trousers, the handle of a .45 sticking from the waist.

Shirtless and bootless, he strolled through the compound gate and grinned into Snow's face. 'Howdy, Top. How's it going?'

Snow scowled. 'Goddamnit, Dobbs! Where the fuck's your gear?'

'Hell, Top. Didn't you know I was the baddest motherfucker in Southeast Asia? I don't need nothing but my barehands and this –' He pulled the .45 from his pants.

'If I had my way, that's all you'd take with you.' Snow turned toward the one building inside the barbed wire. 'Hey, Lightfingers!'

A short, husky marine sergeant appeared in the door. 'Yeah, Sarge?'

Snow pointed at Dobbs. 'Look who showed up without his shit.'

Lightfingers O'Quinn shrugged. 'I awready got his issue in here. The Falcon tole me draw it.'

'Hey!' Dobbs yelled. 'Thanks a lot, Lightfingers.'

'Fuck you,' the marine said with a frown. 'On account o' you, you sonofabitch, I been totin' a double load around for the past two days.'

'I'll make it up to you in the field,' Dobbs said. 'I'll give you all my pork sausage patties outta the Cs.'

'Fuck you, fuck your mammy and fuck your miserable ol' granny,' Lightfingers said turning from the door.

'Ah, yes!' MSG Snow sighed looking heavenward. 'It's so nice to have things back to normal.'

Baldwin sat up slowly on his bunk, gingerly cradling his left arm with the right. He reached up to the shoulder and gently felt around the deltoid muscle.

Out of joint – nothing unusual. It's been popping in and out since that pick-up tackle game when he was in junior high back in Wichita. With a practiced combination shrug and push, the limb popped back in.

He took stock of his physical condition. His legs and buttocks were bruised and sore from the kicks and punches that son of a bitch Nguyen had dished out all night long and into the middle of the day. His wrists were badly swollen from hanging by them for so many hours. He needed medical treatment and hot soaks for those types of injuries. But the best he could do for himself was rest – to lie back on the little bunk and let his body try to mend itself as best it could without external aid. Such time spent would be invaluable if he were to survive.

He eased his sore back down on the mattress. He willfully worked at relaxing every muscle in his body. Then he closed his eyes in an effort to drift off to needed sleep.

'Outside Number Five! Outside! Outside! Number Five! Outside!'

FIVE

Most of the men were engaged in animated conversation, renewing old friendships: 'What's a'matter, can'tcha make it on the outside?'

Reciting tall tales of the latest sexual conquests: 'Man, the bitch was all *over* my ass!'

Passing on information regarding mutual acquaintances: 'Hear about ol' Fieldhouse? Him and a lieutenant named Busch ended up in the pokey after stealin' them refrigerators meant for the officers club at Da Nang!'

Three individuals, however, remained rather quiet. One was a Germanic-looking man in unmarked tiger fatigues. The others were a pair of navy men, one an officer, sitting off by themselves.

All talking ceased the minute Captain Robert Falconi strode to the head of the room. 'Listen up!'

The room went silent, expressions became serious and all eyes snapped to the tall officer. He was the commander – *the man* – the guy that was to honcho whatever mission they would soon be leaving on. This was the start of the briefing and each detail had to be absorbed, digested, studied, questioned, poked and prodded until every swinging dick in the detachment knew his job inside and out.

Then he could start learning his buddy's.

'Nice to have you crazy bastards in the same room again,' Falconi said. 'SOG's laying another one on us, and it's going to be hairy and precise. The mission is – to raid a prison camp in North Vietnam, rescue the five prisoners held there, capture two wanted bad guys and get out.' He paused to make sure it had sunk in. 'Sergeant Snow will give you the execution phase of the briefing.'

The tall NCO, the senior of the enlisted men, took the Falcon's place and slammed his pointer between them on the wall map. 'There's where it is,' he began. 'In the northwest corner of North Vietnam between the Chinese and Laotian borders. And you are at D minus two days. We will leave this air base aboard an Air America C-130 at 0130 hours on D-Day. First call will be on D minus One at 2300 hours, chow at 2330, and assembly at 2400. That will be with all your gear – don't lose yours, Dobbs, you silly bastard!'

There was laughter and the supplyman, Lightfingers O'Quinn glared at the soldier.

'We'll draw chutes – T10s – at 0030 and have a rigger check 15 minutes after that. Station time is 0100. Jump time at 0530, at dawn's early light. You'll be able to see the drop zone, boys. Any questions so far?'

'Is there gonna be a pathfinder group?' one man asked.

'Not a chance,' Snow said. 'Until we get there, the only folks in that area are gonna be unfriendlies. The drop zone is here –' He pointed to it on the map. '– which is fifteen klicks away from the objective. Don't worry, you'll be able to study 1:50,000 maps later. We'll move into the attack position here –' Another point at the map. '– and we should arrive at approximately 2100 or 2200. The assault will begin at 0430 hours and should be wrapped up within one hour. The attack phase will be carried out in more detail on the sand table and each of you will have specific assignments. After the raid, we'll haul ass back to the DZ, call in the choppers and exfiltrate, with prisoners and the two baddies, to the B Team base camp in the Khe Sahn area. And while you're there, you might as well get used to it. Part of it is being turned over to the Black Eagles, so you turkeys can forget living in Saigon any more between missions.'

'*What!*' Archie Dobbs' voice registered his shock, outrage and grief.

Snow grinned. 'It'll be good for you, Dobbs. Being out in the boonies will clear that fucked up head of yours.'

'But . . . but . . . what about R&R?' Dobbs wanted to know.

The top sergeant's grin widened. 'I'll be running that roster. And you'll find it to your distinct advantage if you keep me in a good, good mood.'

The others in the room, with the exception of the three strangers, enjoyed wild laughter at Dobbs' expense.

'Any questions? There shouldn't be at this point,' Snow said.

'Now I'll turn you over to Sergeant Galchaser for the S2 portion of the briefing. Horny?'

Sergeant First Class Jack Galchaser went to the front of the room. Nicknamed Horny, Galchaser was a Cherokee Indian from Oklahoma. An expert aerial photo interpreter, he was a barrel chester six feet, two inches tall. Flinty hard black eyes and a hawk nose advertised his racial ancestry. 'Okay, guys, here's the enemy situation. The only troops in the area is the guard detachment at the prison and the village militia in the hamlet of Phu Tong. Because of the terrain and the surprise of our attack, we expect to be able to deal with them effectively. I've made up some overlays to go over the maps to give unit locations. The guards are a second rate bunch made up of rejects from line duty. Most are young, inexperienced kids – but they're armed and, I assume, have had some instruction on using their weapons. Don't take 'em too lightly. The platoon-sized militia unit made up of local farmers with only rudimentary military experience. No real threat there. But we can expect them to join the fray once this thing goes down. Now I have some photos of the prisoners and the two wanted men for each of you along with bios of 'em. Study 'em well, know who each and ever'one is. I'll be grilling you hard during the briefback. The first five are the good guys we are to rescue. The last two are the two sonofabitches we're supposed to take with us. So let's get to know their faces better'n we know our ol' lady's asses – or even better'n we all know Dobbs' old lady's ass.'

'You're fucking funny, Galchaser,' Dobbs said. He was beginning to tire of being the center of attention. He consoled himself with the knowledge that once out in the boonies, the entire mission, and the men's lives, would depend on his skills and instincts for land navigation.

'Okay,' Galchaser. 'I've also got some aerial photos of the area to pass out, and while I'm doing it I want you to meet our asset. His name is Bruno Hosteins and I know you're gonna be as impressed with him as I am. He's ex-French Foreign Legion, ten years' service, who not only fought at Dien Bien Phu but evaded capture afterward. He built the prison we're going to visit – it was a fort then – and he's chased other folks, and has had them chase him, all over the country we're gonna visit.' He motioned to the German. 'Mister Hosteins.'

Hosteins stood up and was surprised by the heavy applause he received from the younger men. He walked to the front of the room, looking stern and severe. 'The area you are going into is full of heavily jungled ravines and mountains,' he said in perfect English despite a combination French-German accent. 'There are all types of good concealment available for you – and, unfortunately for the enemy too. Ambush, while easy to set up for yourself, is always a constant danger. I will show you more at the sandtable. Thank you.'

Galchaser waited until he had sat down. 'This here sandtable, by the way, is probably one o' the best you'll ever see. Mister Hosteins here made it up and I checked with the aerial photos. Hell, he hadn't seen the fucking place in ten years and he still knows ever' crevice and pimple on the land. So study it good, boys. Now I'll turn things over to Malpractice for the medical briefing.'

Sergeant First Class Malcomb McCorkel – Malpractice to the team – didn't bother to go to the front. 'Not much to say you don't already know. You're familiar with the insects, plants, animals and creepy crawly things to avoid. I got water purification tablets. And, goddamnit, *use 'em!* I don't want to have to carry your silly asses outta there, got it? And that goes for footpowder and salt tablets too. Now we may have problems with the people we're pulling outta that jailhouse. We got a navy Lieutenant – that's same as a army captain – Thompson from the SEALS. And that's Hospital Corpsman Littleton with him. He's been with the marines and knows his way around the boonies. They'll be giving you specific instructions on any special handling of rescued prisoners later to those of you that're gonna be detailed to lend 'em a hand. That's the medical briefing. Here's Culpepper for the engineer's bit.'

Culpepper, a rangy black man of some 27 years of age, almost as tall as Snow, took the floor. 'Nothin' much, guys, except to tell you we'll be takin' some claymores in case they're needed. I'll pass em' out. There ain't no big demo deal on this one.' He sat down, then stood up. 'Whoops, almost forgot the Gyrene! Here's our own Lightfingers O'Quinn with the supply shit.'

O'Quinn stayed at his place off to the side. One of the hardest workers in the detachment, he was also the most independent. A natural born scrounger and deal-maker, his heavyset physique was the result of a genuine fondness for eating, but his time with the marine's Force Recon and the Black Eagles had kept him in perfect physical condition. He was still angry about having to haul Archie Dobbs' equipment around with his own, and he gave his quick briefing in a surly tone. 'There's no exotic equipment for you shitheads – hell, you'd just break it anyhow – be regular ammo issue, standard patrol harness, that's all. Me and Calvin are gonna be the only guys with entrenching tools in case they're needed. Go in light on this one.' He pointed to a Vietnamese officer seated directly in front of him. 'Dinky Dow's got the dope on handling the prisoners.'

Lieutenant Nguyen Van Dow, called Dinky Dow (Vietnamese for 'crazy') by the Black Eagles, took the floor. A former VC, this compact five foot, three inch, bow-legged, skinny little man was probably the toughest jungle fighter of the whole bunch. During service with the Viet Cong, he had defected to the south after his girl friend was made into a camp 'joy girl' by the regional commissar. 'We got two prisoners to bring out like you know,' Dinky Dow said. 'One is colonel named Nguyen Chi Roi. Same name as mine, but we're not related. Nguyen is a name like Smith or Jones to Americans, so I not ask you to be too nice to him. He won't get any special attention, except to watch for escape attempts. He's tough, well-trained and knows his business. The other prisoner is North Korean brain-washing expert Doctor Yoon Hwan. He is old man, in his fifties, and the going is gonna be rough for him. We taking along extra stretcher if he needs it. He a hardcore Communist, so may prefer to die of heart attack rather than be taken out as a prisoner. Everybody keep an eye on him. Especially my detail. The team briefings will tell you more. Ritchie give dope on commo now.'

Dinky Dow abruptly went back to his seat and First Lieutenant Ritchie Wakely took over the session.

'Our commo, thank God, is going to be easy,' the young officer said. Ritchie, a graduate of the Virginia Military Institute, was a specialist in cytography and Oriental languages. The son of a diplomatic service officer, he was a gangling stringbean with a wild sense of humor and a devotion to tennis and jogging. 'We'll have AN/PRC-6's, Prick-Sixes in other words, for inter-detachment communications. A homing-beacon radio will be used to bring the choppers into us for exfiltration. The call signs, as usual, will be Falcon-One, Two, Three, and so on. Specific teams will be assigned the proper ones later.'

Malcomb McCorkel, ever the pessimist, raised his hand. 'Are we gonna have the same crystals for each set this time?' he asked referring to the fact that frequencies on the Prick-Six are determined by a removable crystal.

'Don't worry, Malpractice,' Ritchie answered. 'I checked 'em all myself. So, if there's no more questions, I'll turn the proceedings over to our fearless leader.'

Falconi strode to the front of the room. 'Okay, I'm gonna post the team breakdown. Take a gander at it, then get off and start your study of the maps and photos. Each team will be called up to the sandtable one at a time for a thorough briefing on the attack plan.' He turned to the wall and posted the paper, then quickly jumped aside from the stampede that swept toward him.

COMMAND ELEMENT

CPT FALCONI, Robert, commander

RECON TEAM

SSG DOBBS, Archie, scout
MR HOSTEINS, Bruno, scout

FIRE TEAM ALPHA

ILT WAKELY, Ritchie, Team Leader
SFC RIVERA, Manuel
SFC GALCHASER, Jack
SGT CULPEPPER, Calvin
SGT HODGES, Trent

FIRE TEAM BRAVO

MSG SNOW, John, Team Leader
SFC ORMOND, Norman
SSG O'QUINN, Liam
SGT BOUDREAU, Marcel
SGT CARTER, Demond

GUARD TEAM

ILT NGUYEN, Van Dow, Team Leader
SFC MISKOSKI, Jan
SGT LIMO, Ray

MEDICAL TEAM

LT THOMPSON, William, Team Leader
HCM LITTLETON, Michael
SFC McCORKEL, Malcomb

Sleep!

Wonderful, restful sleep!

It seemed the most beautiful thing in the world to Lieuteuant Colonel Winston Baldwin who stood, exhausted and bleary eyed on the chair in Colonel Nguyen's office. Songs, stories and poems of slumber kept running through his head. Even the Christmas carol:

O little town of Bethlehem,
How still we see thee lie:
Above thy deep and dreamless sleep
The silent stars go by.

The long hours of standing had evolved to this new system. Hours and hours at the position of attention on the chair until the ultimate collapse and longer fall to the floor with its painful consequences. Then the kicking and punching until once again he had resumed his place. It would begin again, in hour and hour of wretched wakefulness.

There was the part of Sir Philip Sidney's poem that also ran through his mind.

Come, Sleep! O sleep, the certain knot of peace,
The baiting-place of wit, the balm of woe,
The poor man's wealth, the prisoner's release,
The indifferent judge between the high and low.

'You must answer me, Colonel Baldwin, please!'

Baldwin shook his head. Doctor Yoon sat at Nguyen's desk,

where the colonel had been only seconds before . . . minutes before? Hours before?

'I must have more information than this if I am to help you? And I have helped you haven't I?' Yoon asked.

'Yes . . . yes . . . you helped . . .' *Wait. That's the answer he wants. The sonofabitch is going to take charge if you're not careful*, his dulled mind screamed to him through the haze of fatigue. *Don't let him take charge. No, don't let him take charge!*

'What is your unit designation, Colonel Baldwin? Just tell me that one thing. What is your unit designation?' Yoon asked.

The prayer he used to say as a kid. Oh, sweet God, he would say it with his mother just before a whole, beautiful night of sleep, sleep.

Now I lay me down to sleep;
I pray the Lord my soul to keep.
If I should die before I wake,
I pray the Lord my soul to take.

'Do you want Colonel Nguyen to take over the interrogation, again, Colonel Baldwin? What is your unit designation? Tell me your unit designation and we'll let you sleep . . . we'll let you sleep . . . we'll let you sleep . . .'

Baldwin swallowed, his mouth dry. And of course, in Shakespeare's *King Henry V:*

Not all these, laid in bed majestical,
can sleep so soundly as the wretched slave,
Who with a body fill'd and vacant mind
Gets him to rest, cramm'd with distressful bread.

'What is your unit designation? What is your unit designation?'

The voice, foreign, persistent and unidentifiable, kept probing and digging and stabbing, until from somewhere another voice sounded, clear as a bell:

'Special Reconnaissance Squadron, MACV/SOG.'

Bruno Hosteins addressed the men around the sandtable in a clear voice. The resentment he felt at being forced into the mission – actually against his will – had faded greatly during these first hours with the Black Eagles. They were a tough group, certainly different from the Foreign Legion where instant, unquestioning obedience was demanded. In fact, most of the Black Eagles would be discipline problems in the Legion. No doubt spending most of their hitches in the penal battalion at Colomb-Bechar or deserting at the earliest opportunity. *Ach, nein*, these were not automatons, they were soldiers – good ones too, from the looks of things. It would be most interesting for a man who was an ex-*Waffen-SS* officer and Foreign Legion NCO to go into combat with these wild individualists led by the unorthodox man they called Falcon.

'Fort Rollet is typical of the outlying garrisons we constructed during our war against the Viet Minh,' Hosteins said. 'It consists of a rectangular wall, five meters high and a meter thick. The area it covers is one hundred meters square, more or less. There is a small area of concrete buildings in the center of the compound, as you can see. These were for our headquarters, supply and other administrative functions. Farther out, located twenty meters in from the east and west walls, were our barracks. From the looks of the aerial photos, these on the west side are cells. The others are evidently used by the guards. You will notice the barbed wire around those west barracks. That is why we surmise they are where the prisoners are being held. There are also strands all around the outer walls to form a perimeter of sorts. These are for extra confinement, obviously, and not constructed for tactical purposes.'

The men compared the photographs with the model that Hosteins had constructed on the table. Calvin Culpepper, the engineer-demolitions sergeant, spoke up. 'There seems to be two gates through the fence leading to the cells.'

'Yes,' Hosteins agreed. 'It is a custom of the Viets to have it this way. Good prisoners get to walk through the regular gate. Bad ones, the uncooperative ones, must crawl through a smaller one. The ground is kept muddy and stinking with water or from the guards pissing on it. Sometimes they even throw shit down there.'

'Damn!' Culpepper said. 'I sure hope I never get stuck in one o' them goddamn places!'

Hosteins grinned wryly. 'Now you know the motivation

behind my actions that earned me the certificate as *Evade de Dien Bien Phu!*'

The guard pushed the prisoner toward the gate, but this time took him to the one he could walk through upright. He opened it and stood aside for him. 'You have been good today, Number Five. You can walk through the wire in dignity.'

Baldwin, confused and disoriented, staggered inside to be led to his cell.

SIX

Falcon rolled off his bunk and slipped through the mosquito netting. Captain Robert Mikhailivich Falconi was the army brat son of a career officer and Russian Jewess. From his father he had learned devotion to duty; while from his mother, Miriam Anonova, who had fled the Soviet Union and Stalin's pogroms in 1934, he learned to hate Communism.

Falconi stood up and glanced around the room at the sleeping Black Eagles, then walked to the window. The air base was quiet in the night, the lights of the operations tower showing on the far side of the field. Other buildings, with bright security beams blazing around them, added to the illumination that glowed on the low clouds.

'Can't sleep, Skipper?'

Falcon looked toward the door where Archie Dobbs stood his turn at guard. He joined him and glanced out that way. 'I feel restless,' the Falcon said.

Dobbs whistled low. 'That's a bad sign. I'm almost tempted to turn the other guys out.' He joined his commander in surveying the area through the door's window. 'That instinct of yours ain't let us down yet.'

There was a sound of rustling netting, and a pair of big feet padded over toward them. Master Sergeant John Snow yawned. 'What're you two doin' up and around?'

'The skipper's nervous, Top,' Dobbs said in a serious tone.

'Shit!' Snow stooped and glanced out the window.

'Quiet out there,' the Falcon said. 'I'm probably just getting goosey in my old age.'

'I'm taking out a patrol,' Snow announced.

'Where? Out there?' Dobbs asked.

'O'course *out there*,' Snow said sarcastically. 'What the hell you think I'm gonna do, take 'em to Albuquerque?'

'Watch that ARVN unit, Top,' Dobbs said ignoring the sarcasm. 'They're a bunch o' trigger happy bastards.'

'Why don't you forget it, John?' the Falcon said. 'I'm just nervous because of the mission.'

'Them hairs on the back o'your neck have been real accurate in the past,' Snow said walking away. He went to several bunks and shook the men awake with one word: 'Patrol.'

Within moments Horny Galchaser, Jack Culpepper and Lightfingers O'Quinn stood fully dressed in patrol gear with M16s and bandoleers of ammo.

'What the fuck we goin' on patrol out here for,' Horny demanded.

'The Falcon feels restless,' Dobbs explained.

'Oh, Jesus!'

Lightfingers pulled back on the charging handle of his weapon. 'It's gonna get hairy around here.'

Snow, now attired like the other three, called them together. 'It's darker'n shit out there and them god-damned lights on the buildings are gonna play hell with our visual purple,' he said. 'So let's stay in sight of each other. We'll do the Georgia High Step all around the wire with twenty-five meters out.'

'Can I go with you?' Dobbs asked.

'No, goddamnit, you're on guard,' Snow snapped. 'Don't you even remember your goddamn General Orders, for Chrissake!'

'Sure,' Dobbs said. Then he laughed and said, '*To walk my post in a military manner – and take no shit off the comp'ny comman'er!*'

'Fun-ny,' Snow said. 'You stay here at your post and keep your eye out for us. If any shit breaks loose – and it probably will – you'll have to cover us.'

'I feel silly about this,' the Falcon said.

'I sure as hell don't!' Lightfingers said. 'Them instincts of yours don't lie, Falcon.'

'C'mon, big team,' Snow said. He opened the door at the same time the world roared into life in a blaze of flashing lights and roar of automatic weapons.

Several rounds slapped into the building and the Falcon, Dobbs and the patrol went to the deck.

An incredible half a minute passed before the ARVN security unit replied to the attack. A couple of mortars crumped and a heavy .50 calibre Browning chunk-chunked, sending tracers streaking through the night. The mortars were laid and aimed for pre-arranged targets and their first rounds fell outside the defense perimeter in the proper fashion. They managed to fire another salvo before a tremendous explosion silenced them.

'Some crazy-assed Charlies made a suicide run at 'em,' Snow remarked. 'Bet they jumped into their positions with twenty pounds of HE strapped on their asses.'

'That means the real fire-support is gone,' the Falcon said. 'The raiders can storm through here and over to the main base without much trouble until security can respond.

'And they're slower'n molasses in January,' Snow said.

'How come they say that?' Dobbs asked. 'Y'know, molasses in January.'

'Well,' said Horny, 'in cold weather –'

'Will you two stupid bastards *shut the fuck up!*' Snow bellowed. 'We're gonna be up to our fucking asses in VC in another minute or two and you're discussing clichés.'

The sudden reports of a weapon fired near them caused the group to duck. But it was Hosteins cutting loose with his M16 through the window by his bunk. '*Aux armes! Aux armes!*' he yelled delightedly. '*A moi la Legion!*'

The other Eagles had picked out their own firing positions by then and, in various modes of dress – and undress – manned the windows. The Falcon joined Hosteins and peered out into the night.

'You have definite targets?'

Hosteins shrugged. 'I saw shadows moving before I fired.'

The Falcon looked out and scanned the view outside. 'I don't see any now.'

Hosteins grinned. 'Of course not, *mon capitaine*, Culpepper did a good job of teaching me the operation of this M16.'

Firing exploded on the other side of the room.

'Keep alert!' Snow yelled. 'They're coming at us with satchel charges.'

First Lieutenant Ritchie Wakely tried to get some sort of control over his fire team, but everyone was split off or intermingled. And, he decided quickly, in the confined space of the briefing hut, there really wasn't all that reason for unit integrity. He crawled over to the Falcon and joined him in the middle of the room. He spoke in a calm voice. 'You realize, of course, that we're going to be able to hold out for only about a half hour.'

'With a lot of luck,' the Falcon said. 'We got to get the hell out of here.'

'You mean haul ass for the main base over there?' Ritchie asked.

'Nope. The VC'd just catch up with us in the dark and cut us down one by one,' the Falcon answered. 'We're going to have to go out and infiltrate through 'em, then form up and catch their survivors later when they withdraw.'

'That's just as dangerous,' Ritchie pointed out.

'Yeah, but at least there's the satisfaction of getting a few of them before they get us,' the Falcon said.

'I can go along with that,' Ritchie said. 'The best way would be –' He stopped talking. 'Did you notice that?'

'The reduction in fighting? Yeah,' the Falcon said grimly. 'And you know what that means?'

'Sure. The ARVN unit's been wiped out,' Ritchie said.

The Falcon shouted to the men. 'You guys without boots, get 'em on. We're all going outside to do our fighting. There's no choice for us but to slip through 'em. Then assemble fifty meters beyond the north fence.'

'What about the VC support out there?' Dobbs wanted to know.

'Shouldn't be any – this is a suicide run for the bastards,' the Falcon said.

'Christ!' Galchaser said a bit nervously. 'What kind o' chance we got against a suicide mission, Falcon?'

'Actually, not much more than they have.'

'Jeez! You're so encouraging, Skipper!'

Two minutes later, with most of the men wearing nothing but boots, shorts, and ammo bandoleers, the Black Eagles poised to rush out into the night.

'Let's fly, Eagles!' the Falcon yelled. 'Kick ass!'

The door opened and, one by one, they moved off into the darkness amidst the fanatical attackers who had only one contingency to their attack – death.

The Black Eagles had an advantage over the raiders. The VC were in a hurry and had to complete their work before dawn.

The Black Eagles had all day. Each man, acting independently, spread out from the others and stuck close to the ground. They faced away from the base lights, thus their night vision improved slowly, but perceptibly. By staying low and crawling at a steady pace, they could glance up into the night sky and catch the floating movements of silhouettes as the VC moved through them. With plenty of ammo, and the M16s set on full automatic, they were ready to do more battle than the enemy had expected.

The Falcon eased forward along the ground, alternating quick, darting glances with pressing his ear to the earth for the tell-tale vibrations of running feet. He sensed movement close by and glanced in that direction. Three figures moved smoothly in his direction. He waited until they were a mere fifteen feet away then brought up the muzzle of his weapon. He cut loose two fire bursts and, in the milliseconds of light afforded by the shots, caught the satisfying sight of a trio of VC stagger back under the impact of the 5.56 millimeter slugs.

He listened for any groans, but the silence just ahead of him indicated his shots had all been killing ones. The Falcon went back to his low, slow crawl. But less than a minute later, the old instinct of danger sent a shiver down his back.

It was just above him.

He rolled to the left, and the body hit the same spot on the ground he had been occupying. The knife, aimed for his back, sliced his cheek instead. Without the conscious thought occurring in his mind, he realized he was dealing with a southpaw, and struck out with a slicing hammer-fist punch to immobilize the man's arm. His aim wasn't too hot either, and all he caught was the empty part of a larger sleeve, and terra firma.

The Falcon, unable to see a thing in the blackness, rolled to his feet and lashed out with an explosive side kick – but there was nothing but empty night air where his opponent should have been. Then he sensed the attack from his right – his *ki* sounding a silent alarm and letting him know he should go under it. He did so and was rewarded with the crunch of his extended third knuckle into ribs. But a vicious kick hit the side of his calf, sending the Falcon to the ground. He was lucky. That had been a dragon-stamp, and if it had caught his knee he would be crippled and down on the ground at his opponent's mercy.

The Falcon pushed back along the ground to clear some space

between himself and the other man. The guy had to be a goddamned third dan black belt. His movements and skill in the inky darkness matched the Falcon's own, and the American knew that only one of them would be able to survive the match.

The Falcon closed his eyes, and let the universe flow over and around him. He sensed the break in the rhythm and exploded into a straight *seiken* punch. He was a trifle off. He felt the iron grip on his wrist as the momentum from his effort was used against him. He went with the man's movement and as he topped his shoulder, twisted violently and threw his free elbow back. It missed, but he had broken free. The Falcon struck the ground in a shoulder roll, bounced and came up facing opposite his opponent. A backward heel kick connected, and he spun and delivered a wide-swinging roundhouse kick at the guy's head.

Missed.

The Falcon backed off again. The guy seemed to be little, skinny and light as a feather. But, goddamnit, he could snap punches and kicks that could have been fatal with solid connections. The Black Eagle went into the *t-dachi* position – as still and quiet as a serpent.

No sound. Nothing. No movement.

The pressure, barely perceptible but there, alerted him and once again the Falcon parried the slashing knife-edge of a small hand. The combatants sparred furiously, parrying and blocking, getting bruises but nothing else.

Again, silence.

The Falcon squatted down in a slow movement, all senses alert and straining. He knew he would present a smaller target in this low bow-and-arrow stance, although coming out of it would be slower.

Still, silence.

There was no movement, no life force to sense. It was as if the other fighter could move his soul in and out of his body at will, to live and die in a see-sawing manifestation.

A loud, tremendous explosion blasted from the main base giving a sudden illumination to the scene. The man was out of sight. That meant the son of a bitch was behind him. The Falcon reacted instantaneously by pivoting on his heel and going into the *t-dachi* defensive position to take the expected attack from behind him.

He wasn't disappointed.

The kick caught his right arm and threw it up violently, the limb going numb under the tremendous blow. Another pivot, and the Falcon had the guy's ankle in his left hand. He pulled hard, and the featherweight came off his feet. The Falcon threw a downward *seiken* punch, but it failed to connect, and the slithering sound in the grass gave evidence of the man's escape from further attack.

Again silence.

The Falcon's instinct and desire for survival stimulated his *ki*. It took over his functions and told him to spin to his left. The wind from a close miss flashed by his nose and he folded a knee and lunged forward.

It connected!

A vicious, cross-body *shuto* punch sent the edge of his hand slashing into the man's neck. Then another! Another! The vertebrae under that small skull popped and cracked, the spinal cord was severed and a sudden, undeniable sound of the body plopping to the ground told the story.

The fight was over.

By then small arms fire toward the main base, which had been building up into a wild crescendo, died down – then ceased. The battle of that night had ended.

The Falcon, sore and exhausted, slumped to the ground beside his victim. The sun, barely showing on the eastern horizon, eased up at a snail's pace. But finally there was enough light that the Falcon could get a good look at the fighter who had been so skilled and invisible in the dark. He reached out and rolled over the small figure in the growing light, the black Viet Cong uniform too large for a good fit.

Damn! She had been one hell of a fighter!

SEVEN

THE CODE OF CONDUCT

I I am an American fighting man. I serve in the forces which guard my country and our way of life. I am prepared to give my life in their defense.

II I will never surrender of my own free will. If in command I will never surrender my men while they still have the means to resist.

III If I am captured I will continue to resist by all means available. I will make every effort to escape and aid others to escape. I will accept neither parole nor special favors from the enemy.

IV If I become a prisoner of war, I will keep faith with my fellow prisoners. I will give no information or take part in any action which might be harmful to my comrades. If I am senior, I will take command. If not I will obey the lawful orders of those appointed over me and will back them up in every way.

V When questioned, should I become a prisoner of war, I am bound to give only name, rank, service number and date of birth. I will evade answering further questions to the utmost of my ability. I will make no oral or written statements disloyal to my country and its allies or harmful to their cause.

VI I will never forget that I am an American fighting man, responsible for my actions, and dedicated to the principles which made my country free. I will trust in my God and the United States of America.

Staff Sergeant Marvin Dayton knew the *Code of Conduct* by heart. He had learned it during his first hitch when he'd been a young paratrooper in the 82nd Airborne Division back in the mid 1950s.

After a three-year hitch, Dayton had taken his discharge and gone back home to Des Moines. He'd saved some money in Soldiers Deposit during the service and, without the benefit of the G.I. Bill (he just missed it by enlisting a couple of months past the expiration date of January 1955), he planned on attending college using that money and whatever else he could earn at part-time jobs. His educational ambition was to secure a degree in American History, and pursue a career as a historical writer. Dayton pictured himself producing revealing, outstanding books after months – or even years – of painstaking investigation and plowing through archives and documents digging out controversial historical facts that cleared the record and put America's true story into its proper perspective. The young man sincerely believed that through the truthful understanding of the past – the failures and the triumphs – those lessons could be applied to the future to benefit the United States in all areas, whether industrial, judicial, executive government or whatever.

The ex-paratrooper entered a small state university filled with enthusiasm, ambition and a drive to excel. But he found a truth of American university life there. Before the lowly underclassman got to get into the really interesting, stimulating area of his interest, he had to go through the tedious, boring grind of the freshman and sophomore programs. For an impatient young man who had just spent three adventurous years leaping from airplanes and travelling about the world on various training missions and exercises, the ordeal proved unbearable. Shallow minded kids whose families could afford to buy them college deferments and keep them from the draft, clogged the classrooms and the system while intellectucally befuddled, yet clever and quick-minded Keepers of the Flame in the liberal arts displayed arrogance and smugness despite the fact most didn't conduct their work or research at the skill levels demanded of apprentice barbers.

Marvin Dayton became fed up and he remembered the days

of excitement he had known in the army before. And his ambitions evolved to reflect his new attitude. He didn't need a goddamned degree to write or research history – all that gave him were some letters to put after his name. Dayton decided to return to the military and experience some of the heady changes going on in the world which the United States Army was participating in. His plan was to pull one more three year hitch as an enlisted man. This time in Special Forces. That demanding unit, with its combination of high mental-and-physical requirements, would not only give him a chance to get a real look at the world, but would drive away the cobwebs that higher education had spun across his mind.

Dayton re-enlisted in 1960 and spent the next three years with the 10th Special Forces in Germany as a commo expert. The end of that hitch found him wrapped up tightly in the Green Berets and this time he opted for six more years of it. Staff Sergeant Dayton, by then, had to admit to himself he had become a professional soldier.

His next duty assignment was with an advisory group in Viet Nam. Now he added Vietnamese to his language skills – he was already fluent in German with a working knowledge of Hungarian and Russian – and further crosstraining had gotten him MOS's in light weapons and engineering.

Dayton engaged in several small, but deadly, combat situations, and his battle experience culminated at a place called Ap Bac in South Vietnam during January 1963. The operation was supposed to have been a piece of cake – a quick hit against a company of VC guarding a communications station. The ARVN commanders committed an attack force made up of armored, ranger and infantry units assisted by helicopters. There were 51 American advisors along to add their expertise to the effort.

The first thing the attackers discovered was, that instead of the company-sized enemy unit they expected, there was a whole battalion. Within a very short time, five of the helicopters – all American – were destroyed. The American advisors noted that their ARVN comrades still had numerical and weapons superiority over the enemy. They advised an all-out commitment to the assault, but the South Vietnamese officers hesitated. Their government was putting on plenty of pressure to avoid casualties as much as possible. Their timid and half-hearted efforts not only allowed the Viet Cong to escape that night, but caused needless deaths in their own forces.

Of the American advisers, three were killed and one was captured – Staff Sergeant Marvin Dayton.

His first months in captivity were rugged. Constantly moved from place to place by his captors, subjected to the most rudimentary and brutal field interrogation, and inadequately fed, Dayton put the *Code of Conduct* into effect. He wouldn't answer their questions, sign their statements or cooperate in any manner. The result was that his physical condition slowly but surely deteriorated until he was near death.

Finally, even in the throes of mental confusion, Dayton realized the *Code of Conduct* wasn't working worth a damn. He had nearly allowed the Viet Cong to destroy him without gaining a thing. There had been a couple of opportunities to escape, but he'd been in no physical condition to do so. However, if before he had said what they wanted and signed what they wanted, he not only would have been able to haul ass and get back to friendly lines with lots of intelligence on their methods of operation and locations of various camps, he would also have been back at work fighting the sons of bitches once again – and even more effectively than before.

Finally, for a reason he could only assume was to fatten him up for some propaganda, he had been hauled to Garrison Three and turned over to Colonel Nguyen and Doctor Yoon. Since any tactical or strategic knowledge he might have was completely obsolete, the Communist concentrated on 're-educating' Sergeant Dayton. Special instructors and commissars visited Garrison Three to begin a program of turning the Green Beret into at least a sympathizer if not an all-out Red. This time, he responded to them in a way that would suit them and he suffered no more lack of food or physical mistreatment – and his strength grew. The only part of the code that Dayton would subscribe to by then was the sentences which stated: . . . *I will keep faith with my fellow prisoners. I will give no information or take part in any action which might be harmful to my comrades.*

When the new prisoner arrived and was placed in the cell next to him, Dayton had taken every opportunity to watch him from his cell window and try to figure out what was going on. When he saw the man taking the same abuse he had taken by refusing to salute the North Vietnamese flag, he had advised him to go ahead and salute. STAY HEALTHY. Don't rat on your fellow prisoners, of course, but do everything else to keep or gain strength.

Dayton, with hardly any thought in his head beyond escape, still had time to plan his first historical work. It would involve American POWs in the Far East, and he had already formed the last sentence of the book:

In order to spare American prisoners much of the physically debilitating ordeal they face, the United States Government, at the start of any conflict, should issue a statement which says that all American servicemen are instructed to sign any document or make any statement the enemy requires of them. Thus negating any propaganda value to the opposing side.

Major Dai Vo of the North Vietnamese regular army was ecstatic as he watched his command, the 327th Infantry Battalion, load onto the Polish Lublin 2-1/2 ton trucks lined up in convoy formation in front of the unit's barracks in Hanoi.

The battalion commissar, Major Hieu Lo Ren, standing beside the young commander, turned and smiled at him. 'This is a great honor for us, Comrade Major.'

'Of course, Comrade Commissar,' Dai agreed. 'The high standards and vigorous training schedules imposed on our battalion has assured us this most historic spot in socialism's struggle in Vietnam.'

'Within three months we will be in the south fighting the Americans and their lackeys,' the commissar said. 'And it is most significant where we are to train in preparation for this mission.'

'Yes,' Dai said smiling. 'Our final maneuver phase shall be just north of Dien Bien Phu. The site of our greatest victory against the French imperialists and their mercenaries.'

'Will our battalion headquarters be located there?' the commissar asked.

Dai pulled a folded map from his pocket and opened it up to show his companion. 'We will be almost in the dead center between Dien Bien Phu and Lai Chiau,' he said. He put his finger on a spot on the map. 'We shall have our command post here – in the village of Phu Tong.'

'Ah, yes!' the commissar said happily. 'That is most fortunate for me. My cousin is stationed close by and I will have the opportunity to visit him.'

Dai studied the map with a puzzled frown. 'I see nothing here indicating a garrison near Phu Tong.'

The commissar laughed. 'Do not worry, Comrade Major Dai. It is there all right. I've visited the place on two occasions. It is an old French fort now called Garrison Three.'

'If it is an old colonial post, why isn't it shown here?' Dai asked.

The commissar looked around to make sure nobody was close enough to hear him. 'Because our comrade leaders want it to be forgotten, thus it has not been placed on the latest maps. It is a special prison camp. And you will be most pleased to become acquainted with the commandant. I'm sure you have heard of him – Nguyen Chi Roi.'

'The great combat leader? What an honor! And he is your cousin?' Dai asked impressed.

'Indeed,' the commissar said. 'We joined the party only a few months apart.'

'*La lung!*' Dai cried. 'I shall look forward to meeting him.'

'Yes,' the commissar said. 'Our stay near Garrison Three should be most exciting!'

They turned back to watch the eager soldiers, fully armed and equipped, climb into the backs of the trucks for the journey to Phu Tong.

'You are in your father's study,' Yoon said. 'And he is smiling at you because he is glad you are visiting him on furlough. Aren't you happy to see him?'

Baldwin strained to see, but only a milky murkiness danced before his eyes. 'Wh . . . what? I can't see anything.'

'Oh, yes! Yes, you can,' Yoon said. 'I will help you, Colonel Baldwin. Do you understand that I must help you?'

'Uh . . . yes . . . no . . . I can't see,' Baldwin stammered.

'Of course you can't,' Yoon said soothingly. 'That is why I am here, Colonel Baldwin. I will help you see. Can you understand that?'

'Yes.'

'You cannot see unless I assist you. I shall show you what you must see,' Yoon said.

'Yes . . . yes . . . my father? Where is my father?'

'He is here. Can't you see him?'

Baldwin saw a shadow in the fog that flowed in front of his eyes. It became clearer until he could barely make out the features. Despite the fuzziness, he recognised his father. 'Hello, Dad,' he said haltingly.

'Hello, Winston,' his father said. But the voice was not that of his father. It was Yoon's voice.

'I don't understand . . . it's my father . . . not his voice . . .'

'Yes,' said his father with Yoon's voice. 'It is me, son. I am glad you're home. Where have you been this time?'

'I can't say . . . Dad . . . you know, I can't tell you . . . everything,' Baldwin said.

'Don't you trust me, son?'

'What happened to your voice, Dad? I . . . I don't understand.'

'Are you sleepy, son?'

'Yes, yes, yes . . . so sleepy . . .'

'Talk to me for a while and you can go to sleep,' his dad said in the alien voice. 'Don't you know that? You talk, then you sleep. That's the way it's supposed to go.'

'Oh, yes . . . I remember . . . but I don't want to talk . . . I can't.' Something deep in Baldwin's subconscious sounded a subtle alarm to him. It kept him from following his desires and caving in to this thing that was happening to him.

Time was no longer a measurable element to Baldwin. It simply didn't exist. He went through a routine of sorts, a confusing series of happenings really, in which there was no light nor dark, nor meals or any other desires. Things swirled and made him dizzy, then they settled down into a confused calmness like at that particular moment. It was a peaceful haze, except he felt so tired and dragged out at those times.

Baldwin closed his eyes, yet did not sleep. Instead, he felt himself spinning around – faster and faster into a disturbing vertigo that had no depths, nor horizontals or verticals. He felt as if he were in a zero dimension of some kind.

The prisoner stood drunkenly by the gate waiting for it to be opened for him. Sergeant Marvin Dayton, standing carefully over to one side of his cell, peered out and took a quick glance at the man.

Baldwin was becoming worse with each passing day. The colonel had some sort of information that Nguyen and Yoon wanted, and it was only a matter of time before they had it. The way the man walked gave stark evidence he was receiving an interrogation that consisted of a combination of sleeplessness and persistent suggestion. Slowly, the air force officer was evolving into a vegetable.

Dayton waited until the other's cell door slammed shut and the guards went back through the gate. He picked up the rock he used for signalling and tapped out, H-A-N-G – I-N – T-H-E-R-E.

And, like the unfortunate Vietnamese prisoner in the opposite cell, Baldwin could no longer respond. Dayton sighed, sadly. Within days, the North Vietnamese would have him drained, then probably fix him up enough for propaganda statements or a trial as a war criminal. If something didn't happen quickly Baldwin's chances for carrying on any sort of successful escape would be a thing of the past.

EIGHT

The humidity hung low and heavy in the hangar despite the building's tall interior. The Black Eagles, chuted up, sat on the concrete floor, leaning rearward on their backpacks, hands resting across the reserve parachutes hooked onto the main lift webbing with the belly bands through the loops on the back.

A blackboard, with a hastily sketched rectangle on it, sat in front of them. Each and every man watched the Falcon, standing awkwardly in his own parachute and equipment, indicating his art work with the piece of chalk in his hand. 'The drop zone, boys, and I'm afraid this thing isn't to any particular scale. It's only a twelve-second DZ and we'll be exiting in one pass with ten man sticks – except for whichever one I decide to join as jumpmaster.'

'Shit!' somebody said.

'Right,' the Falcon echoed. 'That means when the green light comes on you *haul ass* outta that fuckin' aircraft. I don't give a damn if your main is falling off. You wrap both arms around it and unass the aircraft, *pronto!*'

'Any obstacles on the DZ?' Horny Galchaser asked.

'Pretty clean except for the terrain itself. It's rolling and uneven so let's watch those PLF's,' the Falcon said. 'We'll be jumping at 800 feet, so there won't be a chance to deploy your reserves in the event of a malfunction. I don't have to tell you what will happen if you're injured on the DZ.'

'That's all she wrote, huh, Skipper?' Archie Dobbs asked.

'Yeah,' the Falcon said. 'Now we'll be coming in on a track of 270 degrees magnetic – and we'll assemble at the northwest edge of the DZ. That will be the direction of flight. Watch which way the aircraft flies off, and walk that way to the far end of the drop zone after you landed. We'll stack our chutes off in the bushes and have a detail to throw 'em on the chopper during the exfiltration. SOG expects us to return each and every parachute gentlemen, so forget about any burying them. Bring the damned things to the assembly point, got it?'

'Any info on the winds, sir?' Master Sergeant Snow asked.

'Just a general one,' the Falcon answered. 'They're mostly light and variable this time of year.'

'I hate the word variable,' Malpractice McCorkel said.

'Okay, left door – Archie Dobbs, Fire Team Alpha and the Guard Team. Right door – Mister Hosteins, Fire Team Bravo and the Medical Team. I'll unass the left door too, so you bastards get outta the aircraft fast or you'll see me standing on top o' your backpacks, got it?' The Falcon paused, 'and I don't want nobody's deployment bag in my face.'

'Which procedures are we gonna follow in case somebody gets hung up in his static line and drug?' Calvin Culpepper asked.

'He gets hauled back – the hard way,' the Falcon said. 'So during static line and equipment check, watch out for your buddy's static line, okay? Get your fucking hands on the sonofabitch up by the snap fastener and trace it all the way down to the retainer bands, got it? And for Chrissake stow the extra in the slack retainer! Don't leave a big loop dangling there to get caught on something.'

Snow, in the back of the crowd, checked his watch and waved at the Falcon. 'Station time, sir.'

'Right, Top,' the Falcon said. 'Okay, guys, let's move out and board the aircraft in reverse stick order . . . and have a nice one, huh?'

'Right on, bossman,' Calvin Culpepper said with a wide grin. Then he turned to Dinky Dow behind him. 'Hey, you watch my static line, huh?'

Dinky Dow grinned viciously. 'What the hell is static line?'

Calvin groaned.

Archie Dobbs, standing at the rear in reverse stick order, looked up at the huge C-130 that was about to carry them deep into enemy territory. He grinned. 'I wonder what the poor folks are doing today?'

The people of the village of Phu Tong stood in the light of the bonfire and dutifully looked on as Major Dai Vo, commander of the 327th Infantry Battalion, and the unit's commissar Major Hieu Lo Ren, stood with the hamlet's headman. The latter bowed respectfully and spoke in his sing-song high voice. '*Chao ong*, comrades. Welcome to the village of Phu Tong. We are honored to have your brave soldiers of socialistic freedom here to train in our area.'

'*Cam on ong*,' Hieu said. 'And we are honored to be here among the peasants. We have not failed to notice your devotion to your role in our order of socialism, as we have also noted the workers' desire to excel during our time in garrison in Hanoi. And, I must tell you, that the soldiers of the 327th Infantry Battalion are eager to train hard and sharpen their skills for the coming fight with the imperialist Americans and their decadent puppets to the south. Only through the victory of the glorious Army of North Vietnam, will the peoples of Southeast Asia know the peace and the prosperity of the Communist world. We are in the second half of our war of liberation. The first part was completed when we defeated the French and threw them out. Our battalion, I am proud to report, is an important part of the final phase of our struggle. And I am pleased to inform you that the militiamen of your village will be allowed to participate with us in our training. And now, Major Dai, the dedicated commander of the 327th has a few words for you.'

Dai took Hieu's salute. '*Cam on ong*, Comrade Commissar.' He turned to the villagers and smiled at them. 'Due to the fact that our commitment to battle is but a short time away, our training will be as realistic as possible. Many of the exercises shall be done with live ammunition, and each and every soldier will always carry a full combat issue during the maneuvers. That will include your own brave militiamen, so I want to emphasize the need for safety at this moment. Watch the children while we are in or around the village, and do not allow them to go near or play with any of the weapons. Even the machine guns and mortars are to be utilized during our time here, so we must all be careful to avoid tragic accidents. The central government needs each and every soldier, peasant and worker. The loss of one life or the disability of one person, would hamper the state in its program. And we do not wish to do that do we?'

'*Khong*, Comrade Major,' the villagers shouted in unison. They had been well versed in responding to haranguing through the efforts of Garrison Three's Colonel Nguyen, who had the additional responsibility of propagandizing the local civilian population.

'And for your further entertainment this evening, we have some moving pictures,' Major Dai announced. 'Three to be exact. They are entitled *Tractor Production in the U.S.S.R.*, *Welding Methods of the Gdansk, Poland Shipyards*, and, the one that is always so popular, *Increasing the Barley Crop of Bulgaria*. While you are enjoying these, Commissar Hieu and I will be making a courtesy call on Colonel Nguyen at the local garrison. *Cam on ong*. We shall meet with you again tomorrow.'

An eager young lieutenant, newly arrived in the NVA, took over from Major Dai. Starry-eyed with enthusiasm, he launched into an emotional tirade as he set up the audience to view the films depicting the agricultural and industrial glory of socialism.

Major Dai and Commissar Hieu went the short distance between the village of Phu Tong and Garrison Three in Dai's Soviet UAZ-69A command car. Dai himself drove them over – rather inexpertly, he had only recently learned to operate a motor vehicle – and their arrival was not as friendly as they had expected.

'Please wait here, Comrade Major,' the gate guard said. He went inside the sentry house and cranked on a field telephone. After a few moments of speaking, he returned to the vehicle. 'Comrade Colonel Nguyen will be with you presently. You are to wait here.'

'Aren't I allowed to enter the gate?' Dai demanded.

'Only in the direct company of the Comrade Colonel,' the guard said. He was a young kid who walked with a limp. Obviously he was not qualified for active front line duty.

Dai became angry. 'You open that gate, *nguoi linh!* That's an order.'

'*Toi tiec*, Comrade Major, I cannot obey you.'

'I am in command of the battalion just arrived in this area, and I demand that my vehicle be allowed to pass through here,' Dai insisted.

Hieu decided to put his two cents in. 'And I am a commissar!' he bellowed in rage. 'Do you think me not worthy of entrance into your garrison?'

'Please, Comrade Commissar,' the young soldier said. He was becoming afraid. He had his colonel on one side and these two on the other, their anger seeming to grow with every passing second. 'I must obey my –'

'*Du* – enough!' The voice of Colonel Nguyen interrupted the guard at the same moment he stepped into the headlights of the car. He strode angrily to the car. 'Get out, Major ! I demand an explanation of why you bully a soldier who is quite properly obeying the orders of his commanding officer.'

Dai fearfully opened the door. He stood at attention and saluted. '*Toi tiec*, Comrade Colonel. But I am a loyal officer of the state and only wish to extend a courtesy call to you.'

Hieu got out of the other side of the vehicle. 'Yes, cousin Chi. We meant no disrespect.'

Nguyen calmed down at the sight of his kinsman. 'You did not properly identify yourselves to the guard.' He turned to the shaking soldier and barked terse orders. The sentry limped rapidly to the gate and opened it wide.

Dai jumped back into the car and drove through with Nguyen and Hieu following behind on foot. He leaned out the window. 'Where shall I park, Comrade Colonel?'

'By the little house there,' Nguyen told him pointing to Yoon's quarters. 'That is where we are going.'

Dai parked the vehicle and got out. He followed the other two up to the door of the small residence. Nguyen rapped on the door. 'Doctor Yoon?'

The portal opened and Yoon peered out at the three men. 'Yes, Colonel? Is there something I can do for you?'

'I would like you to meet two soldiers of socialism, Doctor,' Nguyen said. 'You have been stuck here in your job since your arrival in North Vietnam, and have not had much opportunity to meet many of my countrymen who are serving our cause with such unselfish devotion.'

'Ah, so pleased,' Yoon said. 'Come in, comrades. I will make some tea.'

Nguyen made a quick round of introductions and within several minutes all were seated at the table while the water boiled in the kettle on the stove. Nguyen turned to the visitors. 'You must forgive our strict security here, comrades. But we are engaged in a most important project.'

'May we know of it?' Hieu asked.

'It will be common knowledge soon and, anyway, my organization will move to Hanoi upon the increase of American participation in the war,' Nguyen said.

'What sort of an increase are you speaking of, Comrade Colonel?' Dai asked.

'The bombing of Hanoi and other cities in the north,' Nguyen said.

Dai's face flushed with righteous anger. 'They must not! We will stop them!'

Nguyen shook his head. 'No, we want them to. We can use leftist pressure in the United States to drum up opposition to their entrance and participation exactly as we did in France.'

'But, comrade,' Dai protested. 'My own battalion is going south to fight the Americans. We must drive them out, so they will not bomb.'

'No! No!' Nguyen exclaimed. 'We must draw the Americans in, then let their own people become worn down through a struggle none of them really care about. That way they will be gone from South-east Asia for good. If we simply kill many of them, they will always hover above us as a threat.'

Dai was confused. 'Then why will my soldiers and I go down south – except to kill Americans?'

'The deaths and maimings of individual soldiers will add impetus to making the war unpopular with the Americans,' Nguyen explained. 'And we are in no rush –' He glanced at Yoon and smiled. '– my North Korean comrade has taught me that.'

'You still have yet to fully explain what you are doing here, cousin,' Hieu said. 'I know it is a prison camp of sorts.'

'Yes – with but five prisoners,' Nguyen said. 'But all are special. And two are Americans.'

'*Nguoi My!*' Dai exclaimed. 'Are they spies?'

'The pilot was on a reconnaissance mission when he was shot down,' Nguyen explained. 'And the sergeant was captured in the south.'

'I am soon to fight Americans, and I have never seen one. May I?' Dai asked.

Nguyen looked at Yoon. 'What do you think, comrade?'

Yoon was thoughtful for several moments. The sergeant, fully recovered from his ordeal in the jungle, might be a bit more formidable than the major was ready for. The colonel, on the other hand, was exhausted and showing the effects of being underfed and badly treated. 'Yes!' he said. 'Let us have Colonel Baldwin brought in for a viewing by our comrades.'

'Excellent, Comrade Doctor,' Nguyen said. He went to the telephone on the kitchen counter and cranked it. After speaking for a few moments, he returned to the table. 'The pilot will be brought directly here. And you will see one of these roundeyes for yourselves.'

By the time Yoon had served the tea, there was a knock on the door. Nguyen got up and walked across the room. He opened the door, and Baldwin was shoved through it by a guard. Nguyen took the colonel by the arm and led him over to the table. 'This, comrades,' he said grinning, 'is an American.'

'He is tall,' Dai remarked.

Baldwin, blank-faced, his eyes not focusing on anything in particular, stood slightly stoop-shouldered with his hands listlessly hanging along his trousers.

'What is wrong with him?' Hieu asked. 'He seems drugged. Have you given him something?'

'I assure you that he is not,' Yoon said. 'What you are seeing, comrades, is an example of programmed reflexes that have been input through a careful series of maneuvers designed to place the subject into a confused state and keeping him there. Each day I insert him deeper, until his entire mental process is open to suggestion.'

'And this is done without drugs?' Dai asked.

'It is done by keeping the prisoner awake for long hours,' Yoon explained. 'And he is allowed only interrupted slumber. Never long enough to experience large amounts of REM sleep. REM standing for Rapid Eye Movement, Comrades.'

'What difference does it make if a man's eyes move while he is asleep?' Dai asked.

'That is the period of sleeping when dreaming occurs,' Yoon went on. 'And we have found that during that time certain frustrations are worked out by the imagination in dreaming. These have a great psychological boon in removing agitation and anger. It aids in keeping one's sanity. Schizophrenics sleep very little, for example.'

Hieu nodded his understanding. 'Then in denying that restful sleep to the imperialist, you are in effect, driving him insane.'

'Exactly,' Yoon said. 'But a controlled insanity, in which I am eventually the master and he the slave.'

'Can the prisoner recover from this?' Dai asked.

'Given enough time and sleep, yes,' Yoon answered. 'I have already gotten information from this man by implanting suggestions into his mind. I am able to convince him he is speaking to his father. My ultimate plan is to make him believe he is making a complete report on his official activities to a high ranking member of the American armed forces.'

'And after you have milked him of all this intelligence, comrade?' Hieu asked.

'He will make a public confession of war crimes committed by himself through orders of the United States government,' Yoon said, 'and then we shall continue to use him for experiments and propaganda.'

'How long can you keep this up?' Dai asked. 'Isn't there a chance he may become permanently insane?'

'Of course,' Yoon said with a grin. 'And, working with Colonel Baldwin, we will soon know exactly how long it will take.' He picked up the teapot. 'More, comrades?'

The interior of the aircraft was bathed in the red glow of lights. This color would keep the men's night vision intact so that they would experience no blindness upon jumping from the aircraft into even the waning darkness of dawn.

The Falcon stepped down from the cockpit into the troop compartment. He had had his last briefing with the pilot. Everything was go. He signaled to the men and they began waking up and tightening their helmet straps and undoing the seat belts.

The aircraft tipped forward slightly for the long, gradual ride down to jump altitude. The Falcon checked his watch, then walked down the fuselage from man to man making sure each was on the alert and ready to move into action.

The parachute they were using, the T-10, was a static line operated, bag deployed troop type. That meant it was not opened by a rip cord, but by a line which contained the parachute in a bag on the end. The jumper's falling body pulled the canopy out for deployment. Extremely reliable, the T-10 was designed parabolic, with the skirt being 10.5 feet smaller in diameter than the largest part of the canopy. This design prevented oscillation, while the deployment system offered a softer opening than chutes which sprang from a backpack.

The crew chief, a pudgy Air America man, appeared, walking over to the Falcon and leaning close to shout in his ear. The army officer nodded his head in an affirmative manner and once again checked his watch. Then he went to the side doors and pulled them open, sliding them up to the overhead and securing them. The cooler air of the tropical night whipped into the aircraft, a welcomed relief to the men who had been shut up in the metal tube of the C-130 for so many hours.

After a full five minutes had passed, the Falcon waved again for attention.

All eyes were on him. It was time for the jump commands.

'*Get ready!*'

Each man lifted the snap fastener of his static line up in front of his face and shoved the leg nearest the door out into the aisle.

'*Stand up!*'

They swung out of the webbing of the seats and stood up facing the rear of the aircraft, one hand grasping the anchor line, the other the all-important snap fastener.

'*Hook up!*'

The snap fasteners were clamped onto the anchor line and safety wires inserted and bent.

'*Check your equipment!*'

Each man checked his own front and the rear of the jumper ahead of him. The last man in each stick turned so his partner could check him out.

'*Check static lines!*'

They reached over the man in front of them and grabbed his snap fastener, then let their hands slide down to the static line stowage loops on the backpack making sure the all important opening devices were not misrouted under straps or items of equipment.

The small red lamps by the two doors came on and the jumpers instinctively moved toward the openings.

'*Stand in the door!*'

The first man in each stick swung into the open door and stood there in the exit position, eyes glued on the unlit lamps beside the red ones.

Two minutes – long, slow minutes – passed before the red ones blinked off and the green glows of their counterparts shown.

'Go!'

The men ran through the doors, not slowing, not hesitating, against each other's backpacks. The parachutists in front knew the safety of their buddies in the rear depended on their speed in exiting the aircraft.

The Falcon watched the final three men of the left stick rush toward and past him. Lieutenant Thompson, Hospital Corpsman Littleton, and finally Malpractice McCorkel, grinning like a shit eating dog, winking at him. The Falcon pivoted and ran at the medic's backpack, but McCorkel was already gone into the inky void outside.

The Falcon went through the door and felt the slam of the prop blast against his body while the static line playing out of its stowage loops in the deployment bag above his head. The T-19's big canopy opened with a swoosh and his motion gently braked.

The Falcon checked the canopy over his head, barely able to make out its darker shape against the sky. It was fully deployed – no sweat.

A quick look around for other jumpers nearby, and he reached up on the risers and crossed them, putting the left set over the right so he could make his favorite parachute landing fall – the left side PLF.

His feet struck the ground and he went with the momentum over on his left calf, thigh, side. Then his legs went over his head and he pivoted onto the opposite push-up muscle. The canopy sank in the dead air of the drop zone and the Falcon got to his feet pulling the safety fork and slapping the quick release to drop the harness and rucksack from his body.

Okay, his mind told him, *don't just stand there, goddamn it! It's time to go to war!*

NINE

Archie Dobbs held the lensatic compass to his eye and took a careful azimuth sighting. '273 on the double hilltop there,' he reported to the Falcon who squatted beside him. The commander had a map, oriented with his own compass, spread out on the ground in front of him.

'Got it,' the Falcon said.

Dobbs swung to another direction and, after a few moments of study, sang out, '112 degrees on the rolling mountain.'

'Is that on the highest peak there?' the Falcon asked.

'Right, Skipper.'

Captain Robert Falconi drew a line following the correct compass readings from each terrain feature. He laid the pencil at the spot where they intersected on the map. 'And here's our exact location.'

Dobbs knelt beside him and quickly scanned the topographical features printed on the large sheet. 'We got ten klicks to go, I'd say.'

'Give the sergeant a silver dollar,' the Falcon said. He turned to the man standing beside them. 'The map shows heavy vegetation and some mighty steep hills between here and Garrison Three.'

Bruno Hosteins nodded his agreement. He, like the others, was dressed in camouflaged fatigues bearing a tiger-stripe pattern. He also carried an ID card, along with a set of dogtags around his neck, which identified him as Sergeant Van Wooten. If captured, his cover story was that he was a Dutch immigrant who had gained his American citizenship in the U.S. Army right after World War II. His next plan of action, in that case, would be to try to break out of captivity as soon as possible before the Reds found out who he really was.

'Looks like we're better going off to the west,' the Falcon remarked.

'Yeah,' Dobbs agreed.

'There's swamp over there,' Hosteins said.

'You sure, Dutch?' Dobbs asked using his code name. 'It don't show on the map.'

'The ground is soft and muddy, extremely hard to go through,' Hosteins said. 'The best way is to go due north at least three kilometers – I mean, *klicks* – before turning west toward the target area.'

Falcon looked at Dobbs. 'Got that?'

'Right, Skipper.' He motioned to the ex-Foreign Legionnaire. 'Well, let's hit the trail, Dutch.'

'*Bien*,' Hosteins said agreeably.

The pair, chosen as points and scout, moved off quietly into the dense brush while the Falcon signaled down the line for the others to follow. The going through the clinging jungle was slow, painful and dominated by the pressing, steamy heat that prevented a man's sweat from evaporating and cooling his body. The more an individual perspired, the hotter and wetter he seemed to get. Malpractice McCorkel, in his role as medic, clucked around like a mother hen as he made sure salt tablets and plenty of water was absorbed – the latter after being treated with the purification tablets, of course.

Dutch Hosteins, alert as an angry cobra, eased along behind Archie Dobbs as the two carefully and painstakingly broke trail for the rest of the Black Eagles. Prior to the actual airborne infiltration, the ex-legionnaire had been given only rudimentary instruction on the handling of the T-10 parachute without the benefit of actually performing a jump. The last time he had exited an aircraft in flight had been in 1956 at Blida in Algeria where he had been posted as a *moniteur* – instructor/jumpmaster – during the final months of his enlistment.

Hosteins's reaction to the jump with the Americans was one of exhilaration. He had forgotten the fierce joy of hurtling one's self from a flying airplane and feeling the enveloping roar of the prop blast. Though he did have a moment of fright, however. He was used to bone-jarring opening shocks, and the T-10's deployment was slow enough that he thought for a moment it had malfunctioned.

Yet Hosteins had to admit to himself that he wasn't really all that crazy about the hail-fellow fare-thee-well attitude of the Black Eagles. He was more used to the bootclicking *Jawohl,*

Herr Obersturmfuhrer! of the *Waffen-SS*, or the snappy salute and prompt *Tout suite, mont servent!* of the *Légion Etrangere*. Hosteins found comfort in iron discipline, where heavy-handed supervision prevented stupid mistakes, and the possibility of a disobeyed order was next to impossible. This rollicking group of gung-ho fighters were a bit too independent and informal for Bruno Hosteins.

'Dutch!'

Dobbs' whispering voice broke into his thoughts. Hosteins went forward a few paces and joined him. 'Yes?'

'There's a hill forward of us about twenty meters, see?'

Hosteins peered through the leafy vegetation that all but blocked the view. 'Yes. I know it. We set up ambushes along the trail there. It runs from northeast to southwest.'

'Think we oughta go around it?' Dobbs asked.

'No. But when we reach that trail we will have to cross it carefully. It is narrow, but rather straight giving any person on it a good view of up and down the track for a long distance.'

'Right.' Dobbs said. Then he wordlessly moved out again.

Hosteins watched him for a moment. The American was a damned good *éclaireur* – something Hosteins had learned the hard way in this same green hell where they were now. Dobbs hadn't varied as much as a millimeter from the various azimuths he had shot for himself to follow.

An hour later, the Black Eagle detachment had reached the trail. They formed a single line in the jungle alongside it, spread out and silent. After a quarter of an hour of careful listening, Captain Falconi whistled the signal and the entire group crossed at once into the brush on the other side. They did it instantaneously and quietly in one co-ordinated effort. Much better than the time consuming method of one man at a time, which gave the greater chance of discovery.

Voici tres klug, celles-ci Amis, he thought to himself in the Legion mixture of French and German.

They were closer to the objective now, and every man automatically increased his alertness, holding the M16s ready for whatever the next ridgeline or clump of tangled jungle might offer.

Major Dai Vo, commander of the 327th Infantry Battalion, sat at his chair in the large thatched hut located in the village of Phu Tong. The open sides of the building allowed the humid air to circulate among the four company commanders also seated there.

'Our training commences this evening, comrades,' Dai informed them. 'And I want you and your men to become used to much night work. I know we did plenty of that back in our old garrison during trips to the maneuver grounds, but the jungle here is more like that in which we shall fight in the south. It is dense and calls for a greater amount of skill in moving quietly even during the day. Operating at night presents a special challenge to us. Carelessness and inefficiency must be punished quickly and severely if the men are to develop the ability to fully adapt to this environment.'

A company commander raised his hand and asked, 'Comrade Major, are we to carry live ammunition on these field exercises when they commence, or wait a week or so?'

'We shall do so immediately, Comrade Captain,' Dai answered. 'We are very close to real combat now, and the men must become used to carrying the extra weight. And that includes not only the riflemen, but machine gunners and mortarmen too.'

'What activities will the local militia participate in to help us?' another officer asked.

'They are to act as friendly guerrillas,' Dai told him. 'They are now well instructed in their roles in our training, and will act out the same parts that the Viet Cong will play in actual operations. And, of course, they will also carry loaded weapons and participate in live-firing exercises.'

Another of the small unit commanders raised his hand. 'What about combat loads, rations and other equipment during training?'

'The troops will carry on as though on actual operations. Even the amount of rice and extra clothing will be included.' Dai looked around the room. 'Any more questions?'

There were none.

'Then return to your commands, comrades. I will expect you out in the jungle within a half-hour to begin the first three-day exercise – and remember! This training is important in every phase it offers. Do not allow the men to skimp on the loads in their packs. It must be exactly as if there were going to be a real battle!'

Marvin Dayton finished the fifty push-ups, then snapped to his feet and began his deep knee-bends. After eighty, he dropped to the floor of his cell once again, this time lying on his back with his feet hooked under the reinforcing bar of the door. He performed one hundred perfect sit-ups before he stopped. This was followed by some rapid walking to and fro within the small confines of his quarters until he'd caught his breath.

This was his physical fitness routine. With his cooperation in the re-educational program the Reds were putting him through, he had been allotted a more generous food ration. More chow added strength to his formerly abused body – this, in turn, meant he could expend energy to add to his physical conditioning. Therefore, three times daily he went through the routine of fifty push-ups, eighty deep knee-bends and a hundred sit-ups followed by a warm-down procedure.

He had worked himself to the point where he could perform the schedule even in the hottest part of the day. When he made his escape, he would be moving through steamy jungle, and he wanted to become as adapted as possible to hard physical work in the high temperatures and humidity.

Dayton had gathered several valuable items during his period of cooperation too. Besides a comb and toothbrush (although no toothpaste or powder had been available), he had acquired a rather basic, but useful, sewing kit with thread, needles and safety pins; an extra set of sandals (this issued him after he told them he suffered from athlete's foot and had to wear a different footgear each day); another prison uniform; a NVA pith helmet; some twine (stolen from the commandant's office and wrapped carefully around and around inside the helmet); a raincoat – which might be fashioned into a floating device of sorts; and, lastly, a piece of wire. This was acquired after he requested it to hook on his cell's 'honey bucket' to make it easier and not quite so unpleasant to carry it to the latrine for emptying.

All of these things would be useful for his run for freedom. He didn't know his actual location, but all he wanted to do was get past the walls and head south.

Dayton had worked on trying to get privileges that would

carry him beyond the camp. He was not only willing to go through whatever procedure would require him to gain that ideal situation, but he had made up his mind to display trustworthiness for up to two or three months if that was what it took for them to leave him unsupervised. In the meantime, he built up his treasure trove, each item useful in his plans.

Dayton had gotten to the point where he looked forward to the primitive conditions he would face during his flight. Strangely, he pictured himself with a long wooden shaft, sharpened on one end and hardened in a fire, to use as a spear in hunting or defense. He'd heard of primitive men using such devices and the thought of having one had become an obsession.

Dayton wanted the spear to be at least an inch thick – like a barbell handle, six feet long and pretty heavy. He didn't want to throw it, but to jab and stab with it like a bayoneted rifle.

Dayton's next priority called for a club. A good hefty branch about an inch-and-a-half thick on one end and four inches around on the other. Two-and-a-half feet long would be about right. He had to figure out some way to strap it or carry it on his body to leave both hands free for the spear.

But, in his most logical moments, Marvin Dayton knew his best bet would be to run across a fully equipped NVA soldier, village militiaman or a Viet Cong. Jam that fucking spear under the ribs and drive it upward into the vital organs and let the sonofabitch die twitching and sobbing. Then take his rations, ammo and AK47 and be the meanest bastard in the woods.

Dayton smiled to himself. His morale was getting better everyday.

Master Sergeant John Snow eased through the bamboo grove and joined the trio who waited for him. Captain Robert Falconi, Sergeant Archie Dobbs and Dutch Hosteins looked up from their C rations meals with silent greetings.

'Ever'body's in position, Cap'n,' Snow said. He checked his watch. 'It's 2000, we're a good two hours ahead o' schedule.'

'The guys did a great job,' the Falcon said.

'Right, sir,' Snow agreed. 'Anything else?'

'Can't think of anything,' the Falcon answered.

'Okay, then,' Snow said. 'I'll get back to my fire team. Good luck, everybody.'

'Good luck, Top,' the Falcon called to the disappearing back of his team sergeant.

Even Hosteins was now impressed with the group's performance. With no bullying, curses or kicks in the asses, the Black Eagles had moved quietly but rapidly through strange jungle terrain. Now, with time to spare, they were in their attack positions ready to launch a coordinated effort at the proper moment.

The Black Eagles, tensed and ready, would hit the objective in a bit more than eight hours at four thirty the next morning. Each group knew the job they must do. The hours spent at the sandtable, running over and over the attack had drilled the tiniest details of the mission into their brains. That had been followed by a detailed briefback, in which each man recited not only his own role in the operation, but those of his companions as well. If a man were lost, then another would be required to take his place.

Fire Team Alpha, under Lieutenant Ritchie Wakely, would go over the north and east walls. Their special killer team of Jack Galchaser and Calvin Culpepper would do in the sentries at the front gate, then join the others to hit the guard barracks. Meanwhile the Guard Team, with Lieutenant Dinky Dow in command, would take care of the one watch tower in the northeast corner that was occupied.

The west and south walls were the responsibilities of Master Sergeant Snow's Fire Team Bravo. Once inside the compound they would take care of the camp's administrative buildings. The cells would be the responsibility of the Medical Team under the navy SEAL officer Lieutenant Thompson.

The Falcon, Dobbs and the ex-Legionnaire Hosteins would get the North Korean out of his thatched cottage and hustle him to the post-attack assembly and jump-off point beyond the south wall. Then it was move back through the jungle to the landing zone and call in the chopper for the exfiltration.

'This time tomorrow we should be at our new base camp,' Robert Falconi remarked.

'Yeah,' Dobbs said. 'How long do you think it'll take the Reds to mount a search-and-kill operation against us?'

Falconi shrugged. 'Oh . . . I'd guess about anywhere from twelve to twenty-four hours. By the time the first elements of the

NVA show up at the prison to figure out what's going on, we'll be jumping on those choppers.'

'What about that militia in the village?'

'Just local stuff,' the Falcon said. 'Might be useful for looking for downed pilots and that sort of thing, but when it comes to real serious fighting they won't count for much. Just be glad there's not a regular NVA outfit in the area.'

Hosteins finished his meal and tossed the can into the small sump they had dug. The Falcon wanted them to leave the area as sterile as possible, even though the Commies would know for sure it had been pulled off by Americans. The size of the inevitable bootprints left would be a dead give-away.

Dobbs looked at the former legionnaire. 'What do you think of our rations?'

Hosteins nodded in an agreeable manner. 'Not bad. My old outfit in Russia would have given their right arms for food this good.'

'Good?' Archie Dobbs asked astounded. 'Dutch, this shit is terrible!'

'It wouldn't have been on the Russian Front,' Hosteins said. 'Sometimes we went up to three days without eating. And in freezing weather where a man burned calories just sitting around.'

'Yeah, well, in a case like that maybe Cs are okay,' Dobbs relented.

'They're experimenting with freeze-dried stuff,' Falconi said. 'Supposed to be better. We Americans are spoiled when it comes to food.'

'We used to get in one day in the Legion what you people eat in a single meal,' Hosteins said. 'But, we did have powdered wine.'

'What?'

'*C'est wahr*,' Hosteins said. 'One packet per canteen cup.'

'Could you get a buzz on?' Dobbs asked eagerly.

'If you used enough and mixed it right, but even then it took a lot of imagination,' Hosteins said. 'But no one would waste the time. Besides fighting, the one thing the *Légion Etrangere* is noted for is drunkeness. Most of our old sweats preferred real liquor.'

'In the American army it's beer,' the Falcon said. 'Did either one of you guys ever read the book *From Here to Eternity* by James Jones? It was about the old pre-World War II regulars, and in it he said that beer was the wine of the army.'

'The guy was absolutely right. And that's what's keeping me going,' Archie Dobbs said. 'The beautiful thought of that cold beer I'll be drinking tomorrow night when this shit's over with.'

'Speaking of the operation,' the Falcon said looking at Hosteins. 'Your job is done until we leave the area tomorrow. You can wait right here for the post-attack assembly.'

'I will go *mon capitaine*,' Hosteins said.

'I wouldn't if I was you,' Dobbs said.

Hosteins turned and looked at the man who had been his companion during the day's trek. 'I disagree with you, Dobbs. I believe you would go.'

The Falcon laughed. 'You're right. He wouldn't even consider staying behind.'

'Maybe not!' Dobbs allowed. 'But only because I wouldn't want to be the only sane sonofabitch around here.'

TEN

Beginning at 0415 hours, twenty sets of eyes watched the luminous dials on their watches. Ten minutes later, the Prick-Six radios were switched on and the various team leaders put them up to their ears to listen to the hissing sound of dead air over their commo system.

Finally, at exactly 0430 hours, the hissing stopped and Falconi's voice spoke clearly, 'Kick ass!'

Lieutenant Wakely motioned his men forward. Horny Galchaser and Calvin Culpepper, located in a forward position, preceded them. The two edged to the front guard shack and watched a short sentry, sleepy and bored, limp back and forth across the length of the gate. When he turned to move the other way, Culpepper, with Horny backing him up, moved into action. He got behind the man and slipped his hand quickly around his mouth. At that exact instant, the four inch blade of his commando stiletto sliced into the kid's back.

The guard struggled, but a quick slash across the throat stilled him for good. Horny gave Culpepper a compliment on his work by patting his shoulder. Then he turned and motioned the others on.

While the rest of the team moved on to their objective, the Falcon, Dobbs and Hosteins rushed silently to the small bungalow between the barbed wire and the wall. They stopped at the door, found it unlocked and went inside. Dobbs went up to the sleeping figure on the bed and put the muzzle of his M16 into his face.

Falcon shook the man awake. 'Let's go.'

Doctor Yoon Hwan blinked his eyes a couple of times, then opened them. They widened at the sight of the American and his weapon.

'I told you to shake your ass,' Falcon said.

Yoon stiffened in panic and fear. 'No Englis' . . . no Englis' ' he sputtered frantically.

'Lyin' motherfucker, Yoon,' Dobbs said. 'Get your fucking ass off that bunk, you slope bastard!'

Falcon grabbed the North Korean by the shoulder and pulled him to his feet. 'Get dressed quick.'

'The man said quick, motherfucker,' Dobbs said.

Hosteins, as per previous planning, rustled through the clothing hung and stacked around a corner coatrack. He found a khaki uniform of sorts and canvas jungle shoes. He brought them over. '*Habilliez schnell!* Get dressed, motherfucker!' he snapped.

Dobbs grinned. 'Now you're learnin' to speak real English, Dutch.'

Yoon understood what was required of him. He quickly put on the clothing and, with Dobbs and Hosteins each taking an arm, was rushed outside and into the compound.

Snow's Bravo Team had already dropped from the west and south walls and hit the administration buildings. The offices were unguarded and unoccupied except for the quarters of Colonel Nguyen Chi Roi. He had sensed something was wrong and had already dressed and was on his way across the room when Sergeant Marcel Boudreau charged through the door. Nguyen's East German Makarov 9-millimeter pistol flew from its holster in its owner's hand and barked twice. The Cajun staggered forward and collapsed, his blood rapidly forming a pool around him. Snow, who had been right behind Boudreau jumped back outside through the door. He pulled a concussion grenade from his shoulder harness, yanked the pin and counted, 'One-and-two-and-three-and-four . . .'

The handle sprang off as it hit the floor inside. Nguyen dived for his bunk and tried to pull off the mattress to protect himself, but the compact interior of the concrete buildings increased the effect of the explosive. He spun and staggered with blood coming from his nose and ears before sinking to his knees in a stunned stupor. Snow and Lightfingers O'Quinn rushed in and grabbed him, hustling the North Vietnamese officer outside and toward the gate in the south wall. The two remaining members of the team, Sergeants Carter and Ormond, grabbed Boudreau's corpse and followed, struggling across the compound yard with their burden.

Fire Team Alpha, with Lieutenant Ritchie Wakely leading,

had already reached the guard barracks and tossed in their own grenades. Preferring the fragmentation type for their particular task, the ensuing explosions tore hell out of the interior of the billets leaving pieces of bunks, side tables and North Vietnamese guards splattered all over the place. Feathers, floating through the air from the rent mattresses, stuck to the blood on the walls and floor. Galchaser and Culpepper, with Rivera and Hodges in tow, rushed inside and sprayed 5.56 millimeter bullets into both the dead and groaning with equal abandon.

The guard in the tower proved more obstinate to Lieutenant Dinky Dow and his two men. The kid didn't hit anybody, but he was shooting fast enough and wild enough to keep them pinned down around the far side of the barracks. Sergeant First Class Jan Miskoski solved the problem by lobbing a grenade over the barracks roof in a high arc. The guard saw the object coming and, instead of staying cool and risking only a broken leg with a rush down the ladder, he panicked and ran stupidly around in a small circle while the grenade continued on its way to explode in the floor of the tower.

The sentry's torn corpse catapulted out of the tall structure, turning lazy cartwheels until crashing to the compound dirt below.

When the first grenade exploded, Staff Sergeant Marvin Dayton's reflexes had him on his feet before he was even awake. He rushed to his cell door and looked out. Shadowy figures of men – big men – rushed around in organized confusion, shooting and bringing things under their control. He stepped back when a trio broke off from the others and rushed the cells.

The pounding of leather soles on the hardbaked earth neared and finally a face, obviously that of a white man despite the dark green and black camouflage paint streaked on it, peered into his cell. 'Hey, babe, what's happening?'

'Shit! *You* tell me!' Dayton exclaimed.

There was a rattle of keys and locks in the next cell, then finally Dayton's own door swung open. The armed man rushed in and grabbed his arm. 'Let's go, goddamnit! We come here expressly for you guys.'

Dayton's mind whirled. 'Wait! Wait! I gotta get my stuff, man.'

'What stuff?' Malpractice McCorkel asked.

'My sewing kit, and the sandals and my toothbrush and –'

'You crazy, man? You can get all that shit at the PX tomorrow. C'mon, shag ass!'

Next door, Lieutenant Thompson ushered Colonel Baldwin outside. The prisoner stood quietly, allowing himself to be led around without resistance. Thompson turned to Hospital Corpsman Littleton. 'This guy may be drugged. Start him off for the back gate.'

The navy doctor rushed over to Dayton and McCorkel. 'How you doing?' he asked.

McCorkel was angry. 'He don't wanna leave his stuff behind, sir. Hell, it's all junk!'

'No, it ain't!' Dayton yelled angrily. 'I been saving that shit up for the past nine months, goddamnit!'

'Take him away, quickly!' Thompson ordered. 'Don't argue with him, grab his arm and follow Littleton and that other guy.'

'Yes, sir. C'mon, guy, stop fuckin' around!' He pulled Dayton in the direction they were to go. 'We got boots and tigers just your size waitin' for you.'

Falcon appeared with Hosteins and Dobbs leading Yoon. The two were sent off after McCorkel while the Falcon stayed to check out the other prisoners with Thompson. The prognosis, after visiting the cells, was not good.

'We won't be taking these three anywhere,' Thompson said. 'And I'm not real sure about that big American – I presume he's the air force lieutenant colonel.'

'What's the matter with him?'

'He's just out of it, sir,' Thompson said. 'What're you going to do with the remaining three?'

'Join the others, Lieutenant,' Falconi said. 'There's nothing a doctor can do here. I'll handle the prisoners.'

Thompson, still a dedicated MD despite being a SEAL, hesitated, then shrugged. He knew what had to be done. 'Right. See you at the rendezvous.'

The Falcon went into the nearest cell. He recognized the occupant as Lam Phu the kidnapped ARVN general. The man, dazed and incoherent, sat on his bunk. The American pulled the packet from his pocket and took out a white capsule. He pushed it into the man's mouth then applied some upward pressure on the jaw. The prisoner stiffened, then flopped over on the bunk and bounced to the floor.

The second man, Chin Lau the agent, was unconscious, but the results were the same. The last was standing and talking, but had clearly lost his mind. The Falcon handed him the capsule and the unfortunate individual swallowed it without asking questions.

The final prisoner to be dealt with was Trinh Duc, the NVA officer who had attempted to defect. The Falcon regretted it, but there would be no opportunity for the man to provide any helpful intelligence. He was a virtual vegetable. The American fed him one of the capsules.

Robert Falconi rushed back outside and saw the last Black Eagles disappear through the back gate. He rushed after them, leaving the smoking wreckage with the scattered corpses for the North Vietnamese to clean up.

The young soldiers looked tired but satisfied during the initial phase of the critique of their conduct during the field training exercise. It had been a rough night for the 327th Infantry Battalion, but listening to their commander's praise made it all worth while. Now it was time for the second half of the after-action talk. Like all the countless others before it, was handled by the battalion commissar Major Hieu.

'Your spirit and determination reflect the best qualities of socialism and the people's revolution,' Hieu said. 'When you are at last in real battle with the enemies –'

The explosions broke the dawn silence.

Hieu looked around puzzled. He gestured to Dai and asked, 'Is there another exercise besides this one?'

'Yes,' Dai answered. 'But it involves night patrolling without simulated combat.'

Now the sound of automatic weapons could be easily heard.

'Is that not near Garrison Three?' Hieu wondered aloud.

'I will raise the command post at Phu Tong.' Dai signaled to his commo man. The soldier, with the receiver/transmitter strapped to his back, trotted over and obediently squatted down beside his commanding officer as the latter switched on the Soviet R-108 tactical radio. '*Tong-hanh-dinh*, this is *Menhlenh* – over.'

Commissar Hieu and the rest of the troops listened to the one sided conversation.

'What is the firing in your vicinity, over. You don't know? Then send some men to investigate. And transmit the information to me immediately – out.'

'They know nothing, Comrade Major?' Hieu asked.

'No, it has just started. The officer-in-charge of the command post is to check out the situation, Comrade Commissar,' Dai said. 'Please continue your talk. It is probably only the man on the patrol exercise becoming too exuberant.'

'Of course, Comrade Major.' Hieu turned back to the troops. 'Even though tonight's work was only simulation, your attitudes and participation reflect a strong devotion to our cause and our leader Ho Chi Minh. If he could have seen you, he would have been proud and would have praised you.' Hieu paused. 'But we have two individualists who did not show the proper loyalty or attitude. Both Comrade Major Dai and I have chastised them severely, and they wish to make a public confession to you, their fellow soldiers.' Hieu waved to the back and barked, '*Phan dong!*'

A sergeant used his AK47 assault rifle to push two miserable looking youngsters forward to stand in front of the crowd. Both had their arms and hands bound behind them, their heads hanging in shame.

Hieu kicked the first one forward. 'Confess!' he commanded.

The boy, his voice quavering, spoke haltingly. 'I sat down at my observation post and smoked a cigarette when I was supposed to be on the alert.'

Hieu struck him hard on the back of the head. 'And what more do you say?'

'I beg my comrades to forgive me and I will try to be a better soldier for socialism in the future . . .'

'And anything else?' Hieu inquired with a kick to the shin.

The young soldier grimaced in pain. 'And . . . and I deserve whatever punishment Comrade Major Dai gives me.'

Hieu pulled the boy back and shoved the other soldier to the front. But before the malfeasant could speak, the voice of Major Dai sounded by the radio.

'*Tong-hanh-dinh*, this is *Menhlenh*, over –' As Dai listened to the transmission, his facial expression went from politely quizzical to surprise, then to anger. 'You are sure? Over. Wait for my return – out.' He turned to the troops. 'Garrison Three has been attacked by imperialist bandits! This is not a training exercise, comrade soldiers. It is the real thing! We must hunt down the jackals and destroy them!'

Hieu, as confused as the soldiers, watched in perplexity as the unit was formed up and double-timed out of the area toward the scene of the fighting.

The Black Eagles waited as the Falcon joined them. Marvin Dayton, dressing in the tiger uniform – including patrol harness – that Lightfingers O'Quinn had provided for him, was still complaining about leaving his things behind in his prison cell.

Snow noticed his commander had brought no one else with him out of the garrison. 'No other prisoners, sir?'

'They didn't make it,' Falconi said. He noted the poncho covered body on one of the stretchers that had been brought along for the liberated prisoners. 'Who is it?' he asked.

'Bourdeau, sir,' Snow answered. 'He bought the farm in the commandant's quarters.'

Falconi saw that the North Vietnamese colonel, though still bloody, had recovered sufficiently to walk. He glanced at Doctor Yoon. The old man, breathing hard, looked distressed and very, very ancient in the Oriental sense.

The Falcon also noticed the prisoner named Baldwin had been dressed in his tigers and good boots. Hospital Corpsman Littleton was tying the man's laces for him. The pilot had a vacant expression on his face, staring over the heads of the others without comment or even a sign he knew they were there. Falconi walked over to Lieutenant Thompson. 'What shape is Baldwin in?'

'Not too bad physically, sir,' Thompson said. 'But at this point he seems to be just about one step above a vegetable.'

'Can he go with us?'

'I'd say so, sir,' Thompson said. 'Unless we have to run.'

The Falcon indicated the thick vegetation. 'We can't run through this shit anyhow.' He looked around for Dobbs and spotted him and Dutch Hosteins away from the others studying the map to plan the return. He joined them. Although it would have been easier and simpler to go back the exact way they had come, Falconi practiced one maxim faithfully : *never walk the same trail twice in Vietnam*. 'Ready to go, guys?'

Dobbs looked up and grinned. 'With that cold beer waitin' for us back at the base camp – damn straight, Skipper, let's haul ass.'

Snow took the hint and ordered the men into column formation. Dinky Dow and his men now formed up with the medical team. Colonel Nguyen and Doctor Yoon were placed in the middle with Miskoski and Limo guarding them. Before the top sergeant could order them to move out, Marvin Dayton walked up to Colonel Nguyen and struck him so hard the man staggered back into Miskoski. The Polish-American from Chicago shoved the North Vietnamese officer forward where he received another punch from the ex-prisoner.

'That's for making me a kiss-ass, you sonofabitch!' Dayton snarled. He spun on his heel and faced Yoon. 'And if you weren't such a wrinkled old bastard, I'd do the same to you!'

'Hey, Sergeant Dayton,' Snow called to him. He slipped the dead Boudreau's M16 off his shoulder and held it out. 'Take this and keep your eye on those two bastards. I figure you've got more reason than any of us not to want them to get away.'

'Damn straight, Top,' Dayton said taking the rifle. He hefted it and grinned. 'This is better'n a big wooden stick anytime.'

'What the hell do you mean by that?' Snow asked.

'Nothin', Top. Not a goddamned thing.' Then Dayton laughed at his own private joke.

'Pass the word up to the front,' Snow said. 'Let's do like the ol' shepherd and get the flock outta here.'

Major Dai stood in the center of the prison compound and followed the obvious trail to the south gate where the raiders had exited with their prisoners.

'Can we catch them, Comrade Major?' Hieu asked angrily.

Dai pulled his map from his shirt. 'We cannot engage them right away, but look.' He pointed to the open spot on the map. 'This is the only place in this area that can be used for parachute landings or helicopters. They had come in that way and . . .'

Hieu grinned delighted. 'And they have to go out that way, true, Comrade Major?' Then his expression faded into a frown. 'But we must still catch up with them!'

'Of course, but in the meantime, the people's air force will be on aerial patrol making sure that no aircraft of any sort can get in to pull them out.' He laughed loudly. 'It is a long walk to South Vietnam from here, Comrade Commissar. The capitalist swine don't realize it right now but they have the 327th Infantry Battalion on their imperialist asses every step of the way.'

Hieu grinned again. 'We shall be like the slithering dragon and gobble them up little by little.'

'Yes, comrade,' Dai said. 'Now let us begin this operation. Killing them will be good for our soldiers' morale. It will make them feel invincible for the job ahead.'

ELEVEN

The Air American H-34 helicopter, its auto-pilot locked onto the homing beam, stayed on course, vibrating with every revolution of the main rotor.

The pilot glanced out the window and saw the other chopper slightly back and lower. He turned and looked at his co-pilot. 'He's still with us,' he said through the intercom.

The co-pilot spoke back. 'Somebody better shape up the maintenance program, that's all I gotta say.'

'Yeah,' the pilot agreed. 'It's kinda hairy fluttering out here so far back in unfriendly territory with a bird that might give out on you.'

'Imagine how Roger must feel flying over North Vietnam with oil pressure problems,' the co-pilot remarked. 'You ever notice that stuff like that doesn't pop up until you're past the point of no return?'

'Kind of like Murphy's Law, huh?' the pilot said.

The young crew chief down in the troop compartment chimed in. 'Yeah, guys, but it adds to the excitement, don't it?'

'Jesus, you silly shit,' the co-pilot said.

'Hell,' the kid shot back. 'That's what we're doing in Air America, right? I mean it's on account o' we're looking for real adventure, ain't we?'

'Not me, kid,' the co-pilot said. 'I'm dodging two ex-old ladies who got lawyers screaming for alimony.'

The pilot laughed. 'If you like excitement so much, why don't you join up with the guys we're gonna pick up, huh? Instead o' flying over enemy country, you can jump right down into it and punch it out with the gooks eyeball-to-eyeball.'

'Maybe I will,' the kid said. 'I'm thinking about taking karate lessons, y'know.'

'They can stuff that shit,' the co-pilot said. 'The reason I got into flying was to avoid the physical crap. I don't wanna do nothing that's gonna make me sweat or breath hard – except fucking, that is.'

The kid laughed. 'Wowo! And we been getting enough o' that!'

'Shit, kid,' the pilot said. 'There ain't no such thing as getting *enough*. You can get *plenty* maybe – but never enough.'

'Right on, coach,' the co-pilot said. 'Take another look for Roger, will you? He might've gone down in the past few minutes.'

'Right,' the pilot said. He looked out and saw their companion helicopter. He watched him for a couple of seconds, then the other aircraft exploded in a roar of orange-black brilliance.

'Shit!'

The concussion from the blast hit their chopper and overrode the auto-pilot. The pilot grabbed the cyclic control and pushed it all the way to the right, then kicked a hard right rudder.

The H-34, pushed by the pressure of the unexpected detonation, swung crazily through the maneuver before finally settling down into more controllable flight. The pilot swung back in time to catch sight of the last remnants of the other chopper hitting the tree tops and disappear into the green underneath.

'What the fuck happened?' the co-pilot asked.

'Roger blew up, man! He just went *pow!*' the pilot said.

'What could've caused that?' the co-pilot asked, the trembling in his voice still apparent. 'I'm telling you, this goddamned maintenance has got to be squared away or I ain't flying no more.'

'Right. It's bullshit, man. A fucking aircraft exploding like that!'

'Hey, guys!' the kid's voice, full of excitement, came over the intercom. 'Aircraft at three o'clock, maybe five hunnerd feet above us. Heading this way.'

Both pilots took a look. The co-pilot gritted his teeth. 'Damn! A MiG! What the fuck's he doing out here?'

'I'm not sticking around long enough to ask,' the pilot said. 'We're going back to home base.'

'What about the guys we're supposed to pick up?' the kid demanded.

'You silly ass punk! We just lost one chopper and that means we'd have to overload ourselves. I don't look forward to –'

The helicopter rattled and yawned as the MiG-17 shot over them. The kid's voice, high and excited, broke in. 'He's shooting at us! He's shooting at us! There's holes in the fuselage.'

'He's coming back!' the co-pilot said. Then his eyes widened with a sudden realization. 'The sonofabitch must've hit Roger with one of his rockets!'

The pilot pushed down on the collective and twisted the throttle for more rpm. At the same time he shoved the cyclic forward and went into as steep a dive as he could.

'He missed! He missed!' the kid crowed in triumph.

'The bastard ain't using his heat-seeking rockets on us yet,' the co-pilot said. 'He's just playing around and enjoying himself with his machine guns.'

'Bandit at five o'clock,' the kid said. 'I saw that in a movie once. They called the enemy planes bandits.'

'*Shut the fuck up you stupid little bastard!*' the pilot screamed as he tried to go into some evasive maneuvers. Once again the North Vietnamese pilot trusted to his machine guns and the chopper shuddered and sloughed off to one side, skidding wildly through the air. 'What's the damage down there?'

When the kid didn't answer, the co-pilot undid his seatbelt to allow him room to move. He leaned down into the compartment for a look. Blood was being whipped around the inside of the chopper by the rotor blast coming in the wide side door. He pulled himself back up, his pale face speckled with red. 'The kid's fucking head's blown off, man.'

The next fusillade from the MiG's KPV machine guns exploded into the cockpit, the glass caving in under the punching of the 14.5 millimeter rounds that slapped the flight crew into bloody slabs of meat. The H34, the main rotors spinning lazily now that the clutch had been shot away, rapidly descended to the jungle below, crashing through the top branches of the trees before exploding into a fiery ball of erupting flame.

'What the hell brought that sonofabitch into the area?' Master Sergeant Snow demanded watching the MiG-17 fly off.

'What ever it was, has sure put a crimp into our operation,' the Falcon said.

'I'm pretty sure he hit another chopper back farther,' Archie

Dobbs said. He had been up a tree, comfortably settled into the fork of two large limbs with a pair of binoculars. Now, after a rapid descent to the ground, he stood with his commander and team sergeant.

'What's the chances of calling in a couple more, Skipper?' he asked.

Falcon smiled sardonically and held up the Prick-Six Radio. 'With these fucking things?'

'Then we wait 'til they notice their aircraft ain't coming back?'

'Not a good idea, Archie,' Falconi said. 'By that time this place will have a battalion of troops crawling around here looking for us. That'd be our death knell.'

'Then what, sir? We walk all the way through the north to friendly lines farther south?' Dobbs asked.

Dutch Hosteins interjected, 'I did it once.'

'And you'll do it again, I'm afraid,' the Falcon said.

'How far do these maps of ours extend?' Dobbs asked.

'Fifteen more klicks and we're off 'em,' the Falcon said. 'From that point on we'll go blindly south the same way porcupines make love – very carefully.' He looked over at the poncho covered body of Sergeant Marcel Boudreau. 'But first I want you to get a sharp fix on this place, Archie. Make sure those grid coordinates are within a gnat's ass of this exact spot.'

Dobbs followed his gaze. 'Okay, Skipper. We're gonna bury Boudreau here, right?'

'Yeah. We can't lug him the distance we have to go. And he wouldn't last long in this climate anyhow. And we might as well put the extra stretchers in with him. No point in lugging them along if they're not needed.'

'We'll come back for Boudreau as soon as this fucking war's won, okay, Falcon?'

'Okay, Archie.' The commander walked away to roust the team sergeant and make arrangements for a hasty funeral as well as a long, dangerous stroll.

Dai smiled with satisfaction as he set down the microphone of the radio set. He turned to the other man in the Phu Tong village command post. 'Both Yankee helicopters have been destroyed, comrades! That means the imperialist swine are now at our mercy.'

Hieu, the commissar, rubbed his hands together. 'And it won't be long until we can rescue my cousin – if he's alive.'

'I'm sure he is a prisoner,' Dai said. 'That large pool of blood we found on the floor in his quarters could not possibly be his. If it were, he would have died, and the imperialist dogs would not have taken his body with them. No, Comrade Commissar, I feel that your brave cousin killed one of them. If they are carrying a body around, it is one of their own.'

'And how many companies are out looking for them now, Comrade Major?'

'Three,' Dai answered. 'I am holding one in reserve here in the village. I have requested helicopters and have been told that there will be Soviet MI-4's made available to us.'

'*Xuat chung!*' Hieu exclaimed. 'Then we shall have an airborne strike force to give us speed and mobility.'

'The most important thing for my troops is to see dead Americans,' Dai mused thoughtfully. 'After viewing our murdered comrades in Garrison Three, they must have more than a pool of American blood to gaze upon.' He looked at his companion. 'And I must congratulate you, Comrade Commissar. The idea of parading our men past the evidence of the Yankee's death was dramatic and excellent for the soldiers' morale.'

'You are too kind, Comrade Major,' Hieu said. 'I have been trained to be alert for such opportunities.'

'And I have been trained to direct the killing of imperialist swine,' Dai said.

'That should start at any time, *co phai khong*, Comrade Major?' Hieu asked.

'Yes,' Dai answered. 'And the first contact with the capitalist dogs is imminent!'

Lieutenant William Thompson, MD, United States Navy SEALs, was the scion of a Massachusetts family that could boast five straight generations of physicians. The energies, education and lives of the Thompsons was devoted strictly along scientific and intellectual lines. There were no athletes, brawlers or active outdoor buffs among the men. They were pudgy around the middle, soft-handed and a bit delicate by appearance.

Young Billy Thompson, however, while keen about studying

hard in school, excelling in the arts and letters, and going on to become a surgeon, displayed a slightly different approach to life. In his sophomore year in high school, he went out for football. He had never played before, but had become quite a fan through TV viewing and had decided to emulate some of the players he had learned to admire. Unfortunately, the gangling, five-foot eight, 115 pounder stood little chance on the gridiron. The coach, after watching the skinny youngster getting slammed and mangled for three weeks, took him aside and gave him some fatherly advice, i.e., that if he had even the faintest plans for living a long life, he should stop coming out for practice.

His next effort was basketball. That sport's coach watched the youngster absorb blows from the other players' elbows on top of the head during the tryouts, then gave him advice quite similar to that of the football mentor.

Spring brought the opportunity for the track team, but doing the hundred in fifteen seconds hardly caused the athletic staff to jump for joy.

Thompson contented himself with the intramural program after that. Although somewhat of a klutz, he managed to play in a few of the sports before graduation and going onto pre-med at Harvard. After graduating with honors from Johns Hopkins, Thompson shocked his family by deciding to forego whatever deferments he could sustain, and enter the navy's medical corps to pull his time as an intern.

A couple of years later they reeled under his decision to remain in the Navy. Thompson had found another athletic endeavour to try out. But this time he was more mature and realized that a great deal of preparation would be required. The young doctor devoted himself to a strict regimen of training which included unbelievable miles of not only running, but of swimming. He did all that, lifted weights, took some karate and even got into target shooting.

When the time came, he reported eagerly for the PT test and did his thing for the tough chief petty officer who conducted the trial effort. The end of the examination found his form stamped for approval. Within a month he reported in to the SEALs at Coronado, California to go through the roughest course of instruction offered by any unit of the United States armed forces.

Endless training, running, swimming, sleeplessness and pure torture dominated the training regimen. The course instructors had hung a bell outside the barracks of the students. Anyone wishing to quit the program had but to ring the thing to announce they had had enough.

Bill Thompson, wanting his mates to make it with as much fervor as he wished for his own success, sneaked out in the middle of the night and stole the bell, hiding it until the end of the course.

At any rate, the attempt culminated in the first physical success of William Thompson's life. He had earned the coveted badge of the SEAL.

His mother and father, when they showed up for the graduation ceremonies, stared aghast at the stranger who greeted them. Wider in the shoulders, tautly muscled and with a strong, sure expression on his face, their son had been transferred from a Clark Kent to Superman.

His father had gingerly shaken his hand and said, 'I don't think anybody in our family has ever done anything like this, son.'

Thompson, with even his speech pattern changed after the rigorous training, didn't hesitate in stating, 'Then it's about fucking time.'

His mother fainted.

Now, deep in the North Vietnamese jungle, Thompson stood with his new patient, Lieutenant Colonel Winston Baldwin, USAF. The state of the man's physical condition wasn't too bad. He had been kicked around some, but there were no serious injuries there. What bothered Thompson was the mental condition. It seemed the colonel was drugged, but the pupils of his eyes were not dilated and there were no needle marks anywhere on his body. Yet this highly educated, thoroughly trained jet fighter pilot acted with all the alertness and spontaneity of a conditioned, harshly disciplined dog. And the colonel did not seem to respond to any stimulus, whatsoever. All Thompson had was some simple drugs in his medical kit, but somehow, the colonel was beyond their effect. It was almost as if he were totally insane.

The MD knew what Captain Falconi had done to the Oriental prisoners back at the prison. And it had been necessary, no doubt. But, as a physician, Thompson didn't want to lose this patient; as an American, he wanted to help his countryman back home; but as a SEAL, the doctor knew Baldwin would be eliminated if he didn't snap out of the near walking catatonic state he was in.

Archie Dobbs eased back into the vegetation and headed for the spot where he was supposed to meet up with Dutch Hosteins. He moved silently and slowly through the jungle. Sweat flowed from beneath the narrow-brimmed tiger hat. He had tied an OD colored kerchief around his head to keep the stinging perspiration out of his eyes. The ex-legionnaire was waiting for him when he arrived.

'I went a hundred meters down, and kept seeing the same thing,' Dobbs said. 'What about you?'

'*Ja*, me too,' Hosteins said. 'We'd better tell *le capitaine*. And he won't like it.'

'I ain't exactly thrilled myself, Dutch,' Dobbs said leading the way back toward the waiting detachment.

Captain Robert Falconi, back with the rest of the detachment, waited lethargically for the scouts while he smoked and surveyed the prisoners. Colonel Nguyen, grim-faced and angry, did little to conceal the hatred he felt for his captors. Doctor Yoon Hwan, on the other hand, sat in dejected silence, his head bowed as if in shame. Now and then he would have a short spell of rapid, shallow breathing and rub his chest. If the feeble old bastard had a heart attack he would end up in the same kind of grave as Boudreau – an unmarked hole deep in the jungle.

The Falcon looked up when Dobbs and Hosteins appeared in the small clearing. He frowned at their appearance. 'You two look like you've been staring into the jaws of death.'

'We have, Skipper,' Dobbs said. 'There's about a fucking battalion of North Vietnamese infantry out there.'

'What?' Falconi exclaimed.

'And they are not militia, *mon capitaine*,' Hosteins said. 'They are regular army.'

'They're spread along that trail we gotta cross,' Dobbs said.

'Looks like G2 fucked up again. The nearest NVA unit was supposed to be an anti-aircraft battery forty klicks away.'

Falconi thought for several quick moments before speaking again. 'What're our chances of going around them?'

' I don't think so, sir,' Dobbs said. 'They're out there waiting for us. No telling how spread out they are.'

'May I make a suggestion?' Hosteins asked.

'Sure, Dutch,' the Falcon said. 'Shoot.'

'I have been in this predicament before. Both as an individual and as a member of a unit during the fighting against the Viet Minh,' the ex-legionnaire said. 'The best thing to do is pull a surprise attack and charge through the *schweinen*.'

'What's the advantage in that?' Falconi asked. 'Sounds like the tactics out of *Beau Geste* or some other Foreign Legion movie.'

'The unexpected shock will knock them off balance, and it gives us a bit more time to put some distance between ourselves and those *merdes*,' Hosteins explained.

'Yeah. You're probably right,' Falconi said. 'We don't have time to be fancy.'

'We ain't got the room either, Skipper,' Archie Dobbs added.

'Okay,' Falconi said making an instant decision. 'Dobbs get the team leaders over there. And tell that navy doctor I want to see him. Grab him first.'

'Right, Skipper.'

'Excuse me, Dutch. I gotta have a private word with the doc,' Falconi said.

'*Jawohl, mon capitaine.*' Hosteins moved away toward the other men.

A minute later, Lieutenant Thompson eased up and squatted down. 'You want to see me, sir?'

'Yeah. I'll make it short and sweet,' Falconi said. 'The shit's about to hit the fan around here, and we're gonna have to move far and fast. I got special orders in regard to that flyboy Baldwin. And I don't want the rest of the guys to know what's going down.'

'I understand, sir. Exactly like the situation with the Oriental prisoners back at Garrison Three,' Thompson said.

'Bring him over here. I'll –'

'Sir, I can handle him,' Thompson said.

'I'll do it,' Falconi insisted.

'I don't mean to take him out, Captain, I mean to help him go with us,' Thompson said.

'Chrissake! The fucking guy's moving around like a zombie!' Falconi whispered angrily. 'You think I want to off him? I hate it with all my heart, Thompson.'

'Sir, if he can't make it, I'll do it myself,' Thompson said. 'There'll be a lot of shooting anyway. The others won't know what happened. I can put a round in his head and that'll be that. But if he keeps up . . . well, I'd love to get him home.'

'Goddamnit, Thompson, if you falter just a bit, you'll both end up back at Garrison Three,' Falconi argued.

'I'm a fucking SEAL, Captain Falconi,' Thompson said. 'I can handle the job.'

'Yeah. You guys are good,' Falconi agreed. 'Okay. Have at it. I'll trust your judgment.'

'Thank you, sir.' Thompson stood up and started back to Baldwin.

'By the way, Thompson,' Falconi said. 'You're as much a member of this team as anybody here. Feel free to call me Falcon.'

'Sure, Falcon,' the SEAL said. 'I'm Bill.' On his way back to his patient, he brushed past Lieutenant Ritchie Wakely and Master Sergeant John Snow who came into the clearing and sat down. Wakely was cheerful. 'What's going down, Falcon?'

'Our asses if we don't pull some real good shit off within the next coupla hours,' Falconi said seriously. 'Now listen up, you two, we're short on time and long on trouble.'

'What more trouble can we be in, sir?' Snow asked. 'There's already the fucking North Vietnamese army between us and the south.'

'I hate to burst your bubble, Top, but it's worse than that,' the Falcon said.

Ritchie Wakely smirked. 'What could be worse than a situation like the top just mentioned?'

'There's a whole fucking battalion of NVA in the area that's not supposed to be here. And they're positioned between us and that fucking trail, that's what?' Falconi said.

Snow's mouth fell open. 'Oh shit!'

TWELVE

The young soldier took a furtive glance at his comrades, then slipped around the large tree and tip-toed off into the bush. There he sat down and pulled a cigarette from his pocket and lit it. He smoked angrily for several moments, his ire directed toward Major Hieu, the commissar of his battalion.

The stinking *phan loai* of a party hack! Making him get up in front of all those idiots and act sorry because he got caught smoking and relaxing when he was supposted to be on post – like now. What a bunch of *ngu-si!* Those fools running around shouting stupid slogans and acting like life was going to be so great as soon as that great revolution was won.

As far as this particular soldier of North Vietnam was concerned, the best days were those of ten or twelve years ago when he'd been a street urchin in Hanoi. The French were there then. Generous, friendly soldiers who tipped a fellow fine for a good shoeshine or for running an errand. He even managed to work for a couple of real pretty *nha tho*, and he'd earned some damned good money bringing French servicemen to the rooms to fornicate with the diminutive whores.

He'd learned to speak French too. And that helped him act as a guide for tourists and some of the government bureaucrats and army officers when they first arrived in Hanoi from France for their stint of duty in the colony. There had been more than just a few piastres in that line of work.

Then those dung-eating Reds came along and screwed everything up. No more hustling in the streets. It was the blackmarket that kept him going. Until his arrest, that is. The bastards put him in a stinking camp where he had to sit all day and listen to the drivel put out by commissar after commissar. And if he fell asleep in class it was another beating and confession. Finally, they drafted him and he ended up in the 327th Infantry Battalion which, quite expectedly, also had a boring son of a bitch of a commissar.

There was a faint rustling in the bushes ahead of him. The soldier's eyes opened wide at the sight of the big man wearing the uniform with black and green tiger stripes. An American! When the young Vietnamese spoke, he did so in the only language he knew to use with white men.

'*Non, monsieur le soldat! Ne me tirez pas! Je suis avec vous, monsieur! Je vous aide, monsieur! Je suis un bon guide – un bon –*'

Horney Galchaser's M16 barked three times sending the slugs slamming into the young Vietnamese. Horny, who didn't know French from a Mongolian mountain dialect, leaped over the body and continued on his way.

Sergeant Trent Hodges, not far away, rushed across the trail, providing his own cover with bursts on full automatic. The NVA lying prone at the base of a tree flinched when the bullets sent bark flying into his face, but he stuck the muzzle of the AK47 toward the charging American and pulled the trigger three times. Hodges took the hits square in the chest, his back exploding outward with the exit of the 7.62 millimeter rounds. The force of the impact sent him backpedaling through the same bushes he'd just run through. He fell in the middle of the trail.

Manuel Rivera dove over his dead buddy and rolled off the trail. He came up with a grenade in one beefy, brown fist. A side arm fling sent it bouncing through the vegetation and into the roots of the tree where the NVA had concealed himself. This time the pieces of bark were driven deep into the soldier's face – along with shards of shrapnel. He still lay there in his firing position, his head a bloody pulp, but no longer a threat to anyone.

A hundred meters down the trail, Liam O'Quinn surprised both himself and the NVA sergeant who was caught standing in the open when the marine crashed through the tall brush that grew just inside the tree line. O'Quinn didn't miss a step as he closed in and drove his bayonet up into the man's throat. The NVA grabbed at the weapon, gurgling his dying agony as Lightfingers shook the M16 with gleeful abandon. The man died, his body sagging to the ground and ripping free from where it had been impaled on the bayonet.

'Teach you to fuck with an Irishman,' O'Quinn said continuing on his way.

Up a short distance from the marine supply sergeant and near the center of action, Master Sergeant John Snow delivered a vicious vertical buttstroke that snapped a skinny NVA's neck like an Arkansas hangman had done him in. Behind him, SFC Norman Ormond continued his advance into the woods. He reached a relatively cleared area and brought up his M16 to cut loose a couple of bursts to force any enemy's head down, but a Soviet F-1 fragmentation grenade bounded off the ground a meter ahead of him, then stopped between his feet. Before Ormond could react, the device went off, shredding the skin from his legs and disembowling him. The concussion flipped him over and he landed on top of his head, then sprawled out face-up.

Falconi, with Archie Dobbs on his left flank and Dutch Hosteins on his right, hit a temporary company command post. The quick bursts of the M16s, with Archie's weapon on full automatic, sent the four surprised men in the hole collapsing into a twitching heap, each individual either dead or dying. The trio of attackers, still cutting loose with bursts that sent bullets flying like angry hornets, continued until they had cleared the enemy positions. Then they turned toward the rendezvous point.

Major Dai Vo, commander of the 327th Infantry Battalion, was so enraged that spittle sprayed from his lips as he screamed at the two surviving company commanders.

'How could you be so *ngu ngoc?* You sat here sleeping and the imperialists simply ran right through your positions! You were so stunned you could not even mount an effective pursuit for a quarter of an hour! A quarter of an hour! I should have you all shot!'

The two officers trembled in fear. They both had begun to think that their fellow captain who lay bloody and dead in his CP hole with his radio operator and company sergeant was most fortunate.

'You are no longer captains in the Army of North Vietnam. You are privates! Common soldiers! And whenever there is a call for volunteers for some dangerous assignment both of you will be the first to step forward! Do you understand me?'

'Yes, Comrade Major!'

'If there is a booby trap to be defused or a minefield to clear you will answer the call!' Dai screamed. 'You will die for the socialist revolution, you idiots! But your deaths will be as useful as they shall be inglorious!' He charged them and knocked them to the ground, kicking and screaming unintelligible words. Finally, tired and disheveled himself, he reached down and ripped the insignia of rank from their collars. 'Report to the battalion ordnance sergeant!'

'Yes, Comrade Major!' They struggled to their feet and limped away hurriedly.

Two lieutenants, their faces pale and trembling, next stepped before the battalion commander. They saluted fearfully. But Dai's words for them were kinder. 'You have been promoted and advanced to lead your companies now that your stupid captains have been removed. Let their fate be a lesson to you. Neither I –' He indicated Major Hieu the commissar. '– nor the party will tolerate such slovenliness in the performance of duty. You must pay strict attention to your duties and the conduct of your men. And, remember! Always be prepared for the unexpected. I cannot personally be everywhere on the battlefield at once.'

'Yes, Comrade Major!' they intoned happily and with great relief.

'You are dismissed to duty.'

They saluted and happily rushed back to their new commands.

Major Hieu smiled. 'Now you will have two very keen company commanders. Out of fear if nothing else.'

'The effectiveness of the battalion is doubtlessly increased,' Dai agreed. 'And you must remember the company back in reserve at Phu Tong. That captain will not make the same mistake as his friends.'

'The Yankees enjoyed a brief victory today,' Hieu said. 'But I doubt if they would celebrate it if they knew they had inspired a great desire and drive among our young officers to capture or destroy them.'

'Such motivation is priceless, Comrade Commissar,' Dai said. Then he pointed to the bodies of Ormond and Hodges. Both were laid out on the trail, staring sightless in death into the blazing tropical sky above the trees. 'Now let us parade them with the opportunity of doing just that.'

The assembly area was in a grove of bamboo. After breaking into it, the Black Eagles had quickly covered up the signs of their entrance by cutting and stacking more of the vegetation around the breaks they had created.

The Falcon took quick stock of his situation:

The Reconnaissance Team with Archie Dobbs and Dutch Hosteins was in good shape. Both men were ready to once again break trail for the unit.

Lieutenant Wakely's Fire Team Alpha had lost one man, Sergeant Trent Hodges, cutting them down to four effectives.

Fire Team Bravo, under Master Sergeant Snow, was slightly worse off. They had already suffered Boudreau's death in the prison raid, and now SFC Ormond was KIA as well. That meant their strength had dwindled to three men. The Falcon transferred SFC Jan Miskoski out of the Guard Team to them. That way, their four men made them equal with the Alphas.

The Guard Team, which had started out with three men, still had that number due to having the ex-POW Staff Sergeant Dayton assigned to them. The man was in remarkably good shape and could realistically be counted on as a combat effective. The two prisoners, Nguyen and Yoon, had survived the attack by being grabbed by the collars and pushed and pummeled along by the men detailed as guards during the assault.

Doctor Bill Thompson, Malpractice McCorkel and Hospital Corpsman Mike Littleton had managed to bring Lieutenant Colonel Baldwin through the mess too. The pilot had stumbled along, but he'd kept up the pace. If he'd felt any excitement or exhilaration during the experience, he kept it to himself. Even at that very moment Baldwin stood slack-jawed and blank faced in the bamboo grove.

There was no time to waste. They had to put as much room as possible between themselves and that NVA unit. The bastards were bloodied now, and it would be twice as hard to slap them around as this first time. Falconi started to order Archie Dobbs and Dutch Hosteins to move out, when Sergeant Ray Limo's excited whisper interrupted him.

'Falcon! You'd better get over here!'

Falcon pushed his way through the vegetation to the Guard Team. 'What's going on?'

Doctor Yoon Hwan lay on the ground, his face pale and eyes rolled back in his head. Bill Thompson, away from his medics, was examining the old man with a stethoscope, listening to his heart. After a few moments, the SEAL straightened up. 'He's on the verge of coronary arrest.'

'Goddamn it!' the Falcon swore. 'What's his chances of getting out of here?'

'Not too good, Falcon,' Thompson said. 'None at all if he walks.'

'Okay,' Falcon said thinking rapidly. 'Have Malpractice and Littleton rig up a stretcher out of a couple of these bamboo poles and their ponchos. We'll tote the motherfucker all the way out of here or until he dies.'

'I'm afraid it'll be the latter, Falcon,' Thompson said getting to his feet.

'He's important enough to take on the extra burden,' Falcon said. 'There's a lot to be learned from that old fart.'

Lieutenant Dinky Dow shoved Colonel Nguyen forward. 'I have a volunteer for you, Falcon. He can take one end of that stretcher.'

'Yeah,' Falconi agreed. 'And it'll make him easier to guard. That means Dayton can spend part of his time on security.'

'Yes, sir,' Dayton said.

'We'll combine the medics and the guards then,' the captain decided. 'Bill Thompson can stick with Colonel Baldwin. Malpractice and Littleton can trade off on the front end of the stretcher, while Limo and Dayton can take turns watching Nguyen.'

Dinky Dow grinned in delight. 'That frees me for combat duty, Falcon.'

'You bet,' Falconi said grinning at the other's eagerness. He went back to Archie Dobbs and Dutch Hosteins. 'Have you two worked out the best track to follow?'

Archie Dobbs grinned. 'You bet, Skipper. After a thorough study of the situation and a lengthy discussion – with a consultation or two with other honorable members of this distinguished group, we have reached the proper scientific and mathematical solution which should prove quite advantageous to our requirements.'

'No shit,' Falcon commented. 'Now just what does all that boil down to?'

'We're gonna shag-ass south,' Dobbs said.

Falconi laughed. 'Then move out.'

'Right on, Skipper. C'mon, Dutch, let's show these guys which direction we want them to take.'

The Falcon watched his points take off. Archie Dobbs was an enigma. In garrison or a city, he was a scatterbrained ne'er-do-well, with a weakness for pot, alcohol and women. But out in the boondocks, in a combat situation, he was intelligent, cool and skillful – the complete professional who demonstrated not only the ability to do a difficult job, but to lead others through it.

Falconi motioned to the rest of the Black Eagles. 'Saddle up, guys. Let's go.'

Clayton Andrews strode rapidly and purposefully down the hall of the first floor of SOG headquarters complex at Peterson Field across Saigon from Tan Son Nhut. He flashed his ID at the MP guard in front of the communications administration office. The soldier spoke tersely into an intercom in the wall. There was a loud click and the door popped open slightly.

Andrews stepped into an inner office and met another guard. Almost the same routine was repeated, except this time the MP produced a plastic card and inserted it into the slot by the door. It snapped and opened, admitting the CIA case officer into a small room. With no visual communications equipment apparent, this was obviously a place where records of a sort were kept. A short, bald civilian behind a counter that ran the length of the office nodded to him. 'Hello, Andy.'

'How are you, Fred? Anything in from the Eagles yet?'

'Don't know. Just came on duty myself. I'll have to check the log.' He pulled a large binder from the recesses beneath the counter and flipped it open. After a quick scan, he shook his head. 'Not a thing. Sorry.'

'Damn!'

'Problem, Andy?'

'Yeah. We're running some ops up north and there was supposed to have been a pickup early this morning. Fairly routine. But there's been no word from the aircraft.'

'How many hours are they overdue?' Fred asked.

'Twelve.'

'Holy Jesus!'

'Yeah. I'd appreciate some personal attention to this,' Andrews said. 'That mission is one we're all real interested in.'

'Let me know where you'll be and I'll get hold of you right off the bat if something comes in,' the commo man promised.

'Ring my office. I'll be sleeping there,' Andrews said.

He left the communications bureau and returned to his nook on the third floor. Andrews mixed a drink and lit a cigarette. Then he went to the north window and looked out into the dark, Asian night. He raised his glass in a salute.

'Here's wishing the best of luck to you, Falcon. And the poor bastards with you too.'

THIRTEEN

Lieutenant Phung Xuan, newly appointed commander of the Second Company, 327th Infantry Battalion of the North Vietnamese Army, sat sideways in the seat of the Russian MI-4 helicopter and stared down a thousand feet to the green jungle below.

Somewhere, skulking beneath that canopy of trees, were the American gangsters who had pulled the cowardly attack on Garrison Three, then followed that up with the wanton commando assault which caused the death of six NVA soldiers and the wounding of eight more. These crimes were enough to drive a true Communist into spasms of righteous anger, and Phung was enraged . . . up to a point.

The success of the imperialists' attack had caused the removal and demotion of his company commander, thus paving the way for Phung's own promotion into his place. Now, having witnessed the results of Major Dai's rage, this young officer had no desire to be on the receiving end of another loss of temper by the tough battalion commander.

The pitch of the helicopter motor changed and Phung sensed their gradual decrease in altitude. Finally they were over the trees, some seventy-five feet above the jungle floor.

The two nylon ropes, each ninety feet long, that had been fastened to the special rings in the aircraft's floors were kicked out. They uncoiled in their fall through the trees to the spongy jungle ground beneath.

Phung turned to the section of troops, some twenty men, crowded into the confines of the helicopter. He nodded to the first one. '*Tiep-tuc!*'

The soldier was one of the former company commanders who had been reduced in rank by Major Hai. In fact, he had been Phung's superior officer. And the ex-captain had been hell on the young lieutenant, carping and criticizing him mercilessly. Phung enjoyed this reversal in roles. The luckless man moved to the aircraft door and looked down. His eyes opened wide in fear and he turned to give his former subordinate a beseeching look.

'*Tiep-tuc!*' Phung screamed over the roar of the engines. 'I order you in the name of the people!'

The ex-captain, untrained for such an attempt, grasped the rope and edged fearfully over the edge of the door. The downward force of the propwash caught him and pulled him free from the fuselage. He frantically clawed at the rope, but lost his grip and somersaulted through the air to crash through the upper branches of the trees and disappear from sight.

Phung motioned to the next soldier. '*Tiep-tuc!*'

Without hesitating, the man gripped the rope and rather inexpertly let himself slide out the door. Once free from the helicopter, he wrapped his legs around the nylon line and lowered himself.

Four more men followed, all rather clumsily, but they managed to safely leave the aircraft and begin the long slide that would take them through the trees and down to the ground. The fifth man, however, froze when he swung from the door. He gripped the rope and hung on, eyes closed and teeth clenched.

Phung frantically motioned to him to begin the descent. Finally, more out of desperate fear than logic, the soldier loosened his grip and began sliding – faster and faster. His palms burned from the friction until he could no longer hang on. He collided with the man under him and stopped.

The fellow on the bottom now had both himself and his unwanted companion to support. He screamed in desperation at the man who sat on his shoulders, but the other soldier had once more become frozen with fear. Finally, the bottom man's grip gave out, his hands loosening on the rope. Both plummeted groundward. They struck a third man who had managed to get within fifteen feet of terra firma and all three landed in a heap just a scant meter from the body of the former captain who had been the first man to attempt to lower himself.

Back up in the chopper, Phung watched the rest of the section exit. He had been forced to punch and kick a couple of them, but he finally cleared the aircraft. Luckily all made it without further incident. The young lieutenant followed. As he slid slowly toward the ground, he noted the other half dozen aircraft, spread out in a wide circle, involved in similar operations. Phung grinned to himself despite the casualties his men had sustained. They would never have had this speed or mobility without the aircraft. And as soon as the men developed the necessary confidence and skills in going down the ropes, they would be able to rapidly deploy and surround any area of the jungle.

Tung ho! The Americans were as good as dead!

Sergeant Archie Dobbs, scout and tree climber *extraordinaire*, shinnied down the trunk and walked over to the Falcon. 'There's six choppers, Skipper,' he reported. 'They're arranged in a pattern all around us. About a hunnerd or so troops are rappeling out of them – or maybe I should say they're trying to rappel.'

'What do you mean, Archie?' Falconi asked.

'They ain't using Swiss seats or nothing, Skipper. Them guys are just grabbing hold of ropes and sliding down to the ground. A mess of 'em have fallen.' He grinned. 'I bet that ruined their whole day.'

'How far up are they?'

'Somewhere between fifty to hunnerd feet, Skipper,' Dobbs answered. 'Them chopper pilots ain't too hot themselves. Don't seem to be able to hold a steady hover for too long.'

'Probably North Vietnamese half-assed trained by the Russians,' remarked Falconi.

'Yeah,' Dobbs agreed. 'The Ruskies don't want their yellow brothers to get too skillful with the hardware they give them.'

'You're right. I'll bet they're sorry they taught the Chinese to fly MiGs.' The Falcon was thoughtful for several moments before he spoke again. 'We might as well keep pushing south. Since we're surrounded anyway, there's no sense in changing the direction we want to travel. You'll be running into the NVA up front there. I'll pull one man out of each fire team to back you and Dutch up.'

'Right, Skipper,' Dobbs said. He went forward and joined Dutch Hosteins who was waiting for him. 'We're going through 'em. The Skipper is giving us two guys for some added firepower.'

'*Zur bon!*' Hosteins said. 'We'll be the first to make contact.'

SFC Manuel Rivera from the Alphas and Sergeant Demond Carter from the Bravos joined them.

'You guys hang loose a ways back,' Dobbs said. 'If the shit hits the fan when we ain't expecting it, cover us while we withdraw to you. Then we'll hold until the rest of the guys catch up.'

'Right,' Rivera said. 'When you turn around and head for us, do it fast. I'm gonna be throwing grenades.'

'Throw them fuckers a long, long ways, okay?' Dobbs said. He motioned to Hosteins. 'C'mon, Dutch, let's show these bastards the way to go.'

The two scouts set a slow pace, stopping now and then for quiet periods of intense listening before once again moving through the jungle toward the NVA troops. Noise was the big factor in a situation like that. Whichever side gave itself away would begin the fight at a distinct disadvantage. But once the initial shock was gone, then superior firepower – and luck – would swing victory one way or the other.

Hosteins had the luck.

The 327th NVA Infantry Battalion was made up of city dwellers, although they'd had plenty of training, they hadn't had sufficient time to develop the cunning instincts and habits that country boys or experienced hunters have in the woods.

A thirsty NVA trooper took a drink from his canteen, then carelessly banged it against the tree he was leaning against when he replaced it in the canvas carrier on his belt.

The ex-legionnaire froze at the unexpected clank. Within moments he had spotted the kid and signaled to Dobbs. Archie took a careful peek, then moved forward in an attempt to see more. Satisfied he knew the location and strength of the enemy unit, he pulled back to Rivera and Carter with Hosteins following.

Within moments the Falcon joined them. 'What's going on up there, Archie?'

'Fifteen bad guys, Skipper,' Dobbs said. 'In line as skirmishers from there –' He indicated an area with a sweep of his hand. '– to there.'

'Right,' the Falcon said. 'I'll send in the Bravos first with the Alphas following. The guards and medics with their burdens next. Then you four bring up the rear. Fight through until you link up with us.'

'Right, Skipper.'

'*C'est gut*,' Hosteins said gripping his M16 tighter.

The attack was set up and launched in the space of five minutes. Snow, with Lightfingers O'Quinn and SFC Miskoski on each of his flanks moved forward until contact was made. The first burst from his M16 broke the silence in the jungle and sent an NVA soldier spinning under the impact of the slugs. Miskoski zapped two rounds into another while O'Quinn slammed out two bursts that were stitched across the chest of one NVA. The Red's companion bent double under the impact of the second hail of slugs. He grabbed his torn belly, the entrails oozing out into his hands and turned to run. O'Quinn's third volley caught him in the back of the head and blew the top of his skull and face out into a pulverized mush.

Alpha Team followed through in time to catch the flanks of the NVA unit curving in like the tentacles of a khaki octopus. Horny Galchaser dropped three bunched up Reds with one long burst of eight rounds. They flopped over like a trio of clubbed seals into a small pile. Calvin Culpepper missed in his effort, but the two sprays of bullets made four of the North Vietnamese pull back and think twice about exposing themselves again.

Dinky Dow beat Colonel Nguyen on the head to keep him moving. The Communist officer held on to the back half of the stretcher bearing Doctor Yoon, while both the Guard and Medical Teams rushed through the 'liberated' zone before it was reoccupied by the NVA. Bill Thompson literally pulled the walking catonic Colonel Baldwin along with him.

One of the Reds who had ducked from Culpepper's fusillade, reappeared and fired a frantic shot at the small group. Hospital Corpsman Mike Littleton grunted and spun. He hit the ground on his back and tried to rise. The North Vietnamese soldier shot him again, this time in the chest leaving a gaping exit wound under his left arm pit. Littleton died without rising.

Sergeant Ray Limo dropped to one knee and took hasty aim. His first shot slapped into the Red's pelvis and turned him neatly around for a back shot. The next one caught him almost square between the shoulder blades, making him throw his arms out as he went to his knees. Limo tossed a grenade in that general direction before continuing on his way. The resulting explosion took out two more NVA, the horizontal hail of shrapnel sweeping them bloody and torn into the bushes.

Baldwin, being frantically pulled along by Lieutenant Bill

Thompson, stumbled and went down. He didn't even display the instinct to get to his hands and knees as he lay there sprawled out in the undergrowth. 'Let's go, Colonel!' Thompson yelled. 'Get up, for God's sake!'

Baldwin barely moved. Thompson knelt to pull the pilot to his feet when instinct made him look up. An NVA, his mouth open in a wild scream, charged toward him. The AK-47's bayonet pointed out like a lethal fang. Thompson came up erect, whipping the .45 auto from its holster. He fired three times, each round zapping into the enemy soldier, jerking him like a puppet on a string until he flopped to the ground.

Thompson grabbed Baldwin's collar and, with his adrenalin pumping like sixty, hauled him to his feet and resumed their wild run.

Archie Dobbs, Dutch Hosteins, Manuel Rivera and Demond Carter swept into the void left by their buddies and continued forward until they met up with the main body who had turned and formed a hasty defensive perimeter.

'Anybody down?' Falcon asked.

Malpractice McCorkel nodded. 'Right, Falcon. Littleton's back there. But there ain't no reason to fetch him.'

'Definite KIA?' Falconi asked.

'Right. I seen him take hits in the side and chest,' McCorkel reported. 'After the last one I could see his fucking lungs.'

Four gone out of nineteen. A mission all fucked up and now with twenty-one per cent casualties. He glanced at Yoon lying stricken and pale on the improvised stretcher, then at Nguyen. The NVA colonel, despite being fatigued and sweat-streaked still looked mean as hell. Next he swung his glance to Baldwin. The pilot now looked like death warmed over.

Bill Thompson noted the Falcon's gaze at Baldwin. He waved to the mission commander. 'No sweat. We're staying with the program.'

Falconi nodded. He had seen Baldwin fall. The problem with the air force colonel was getting worse. There was no question about the situation now. Baldwin was too much of a liability. Anyway, a couple of more casualties and Thompson was going to have to become a combatant no matter what. And that would mean the end of Baldwin as well.

Falconi nodded to Dobbs and Hosteins. 'Get us outta here.'

There was something in the young lieutenant's eyes that made Major Dai control his rage. Ten of the 327th Infantry Battalion's dead soldiers lay in a neat line where their comrades had placed them. On the other side of the jungle clearing were eight more that had been killed in falls from the hovering helicopters. Only one American body had been found at the scene of the battle. But Dai had stifled his screams and rage. He sensed an accusing air about the young officer's demeanor. And, in a Communist army replete with commissars and secret police agents, accusations from any quarter were to be avoided.

'Do you have something to say to me, Comrade Lieutenant?' Dai asked.

Phung Xuan stepped forward and saluted. 'Yes, Comrade Major. We suffered so many losses today for two reasons. The first was that the men were not adequately trained in the proper methods of exiting a helicopter by rope.'

'Perhaps you are correct,' Dai conceded. 'What do you suggest?'

'That we practice the techniques at a much lower altitude until the men gain confidence,' Phung answered. 'Then and only then can this method of entry be used.'

'That is a logical idea,' Dai said dryly.

'And we must reduce the men's combat loads,' Phung continued. 'This is no longer a training mission. They must be able to move rapidly and easily. Carrying around all that extra weight is stupid!'

Normally Dai would be livid at such impertinence, but the mounting casualty toll of his battalion would soon be noted in Hanoi – and that could be most dangerous for him. Particularly in light of the fact that he was inflicting such little damage to the enemy. These things, too, must have occurred to the lieutenant. Dai forced himself to smile. 'Please continue, Comrade Lieutenant.'

'And I suggest also, Comrade Major, that a reserve force be held back to be committed to battle once the escaping Americans are engaged by the main elements. If we continue our present tactics, then we shall be trading ten men for every one of theirs until they've linked up with their friends in the south.'

Major Hieu, the commissar, had been listening nearby. He, too, had begun to grow weary of the results of their battles. And he had absolutely nothing to fear from Hanoi. In fact, if he felt any heat at all on his own neck, he would save it with pages and pages of damning accusations against Dai. He stepped forward to begin covering his ass.

'I find great merit in the lieutenant's remarks,' Hieu said loudly making sure all would note his respectful, yet obvious, displeasure with the way things were going. 'So far this operation has been one great disaster. Not only have the bandits liberated POWs, taken highly ranked socialist officers and blatantly wandered about in our great nation, they are now killing soldiers that have been slated for action in the south. This intolerable situation must be brought under control immediately. We are losing face, Comrade Major.'

'I agree,' Dai said. 'At this point we can take a day off from pursuing the imperialists since they will not be able to move far in the dense jungle, and we have aircraft transport that can carry us rapidly to any objective. Therefore, tomorrow we shall begin training with the helicopters. After one day, we should have enough men with the skill necessary to mount operations against the bandits. The slower ones will be given additional time.'

'But how will this work, Comrade Major?' Hieu asked enjoying putting the screws to Dai. A commissar who manages to get the commanding officer of his unit imprisoned or shot has reached the apex of his profession. 'Surely, the entire battalion must be in on this operation. Not just a splinter group.'

'Of course not, Comrade,' Dai said with strained politeness. He had sensed the growing hostility of the commissar for the previous two days. 'And I have not been idle during these times. My mind, encouraged by my deepseated faith in Ho Chi Minh and unshakeable belief in the glories of socialism, has been actively searching for ways to successfully conclude our operations.'

'Proof of one's devotion is in one's accomplishments,' Hieu said coldly.

'I agree, Comrade Commissar,' Dai said. 'That is why this

afternoon I have made certain arrangements by radio through the area commander.'

'Ah! I understand,' Hieu said. 'You are going to have reinforcements brought in. Perhaps a larger unit with a higher ranking officer than yourself?'

'Not at all, Comrade Commissar,' Dai said. 'I have used the same connections that produced the MiG to shoot down the enemy helicopters to bring us three more of those flying machines of death.'

'Have the operational orders granting us these airplanes been confirmed, Comrade Major?' Hieu asked suspiciously.

'Of course, Comrade Commissar,' Dai answered. 'Not more than two hours previously, the senior air officer in this area has communicated his approval of their use.'

Hieu felt as if he had been outpointed. Dai, obviously, had not been disclosing all his plans and schemes. *Time to become friendly again*, his mind told him. 'I am not surprised by your ingenuity, Comrade Major! Our unbeatable air force is going to help us, *co phai khong?*'

'Of course, Comrade Commissar.' Dai turned to Lieutenant Phung. 'Day after tomorrow you may have the honor of leading the first element of our men into combat. And this time you will be able to call in air strikes on the American gang.'

FOURTEEN

Shadows were lengthening fast in the jungle when Captain Robert Falconi joined Sergeant Archie Dobbs and Dutch Hosteins at the river bank. There was a ten foot drop to the water. Its rapid current flowed through a hundred and twenty-five meter wide cut in the jungle.

A formidable obstacle.

'What's the name of this one?' the Falcon asked. 'We're off our maps now.'

'It is the Mau Xanh River, *mon capitaine*,' Hosteins answered. 'A tributary of the Song Bo.'

'What's our best bet?' Falconi asked. 'Stay on this side, or cross it.'

'We must cross it, *mon capitaine*,' Hosteins answered. 'It is much easier traveling on the other side. The only problem is the bluffs there. Until we climb to the top we will be trapped between them and the river.'

'How long will it take us to scale 'em?' Falconi asked. He looked across the river at the cliffs the detachment would have to ascend. They were at least a hundred meters high, heavily overgrown with dense vegetation and extremely steep.

'Possibly an hour or so, *mon capitaine*,' Hosteins answered.

'Okay. I don't like being caught between the water and the bluffs, but I can't see any alternative.' Falconi studied the river for several long moments. The current was too strong for a laden man to be able to safely reach the other side. A strong swimmer would have to be dispatched to cross first and anchor a rope for the others to use. 'We'll have to do it one man at a time.'

Archie Dobbs spoke up. 'That's gonna take five or six hours, Skipper. Are we gonna try it in the dark?'

'I'd sure as hell like to,' Falconi said. 'But these guys are too fucking bushed now. We've been going since four thirty this morning. I'm afraid we'd lose somebody.'

'Yeah, you're right,' Dobbs said. 'And getting them prisoners across at night would be next to impossible. O'course it's gonna take a helluva lot longer in daylight on account o' security.'

'Yeah, but it can't be helped. We'll set up a perimeter for the night. There's enough guys for shifts of two hours on and four off,' Falconi said. 'That ought to get them enough rest.'

The captain sent Archie Dobbs to pass the word. By the time the rapid tropical sunset had faded away leaving the jungle bathed in steaming darkness, the Black Eagles were settled in for the night.

The last thing Falconi did before retiring was stumble from man to man looking for Lieutenant Bill Thompson. He found him settled into a little clearing with Baldwin. The air force officer had evidently almost immediately settled into a deep sleep at the first opportunity. He lay curled up on Thompson's spreadout poncho. Falconi observed him as best he could in the darkness. 'How's your patient?'

'He dropped off the second his head hit the ground,' Thompson said. 'No telling what those bastards had been doing to him.'

'Yeah,' Falconi said. 'I'll need an extra strong swimmer in the morning. Interested?'

'Sure. Want me to take a rope across and anchor it, right?'

'Absolutely correct. I figure that being a SEAL you can swim like a fucking fish, and being a sailor too, makes you tops around here with knots.'

'Despite the fear of being immodest, you're right on both counts,' Thompson said grinning.

'Good. By the way, how's Baldwin doing? He didn't look too good today.'

'I don't know what's wrong with him,' Thompson said. 'And, quite obviously, I have neither the time nor facilities for a proper examination.'

'What are his chances of improved performance?'

'I can't answer that,' Thompson said. 'We'll have to wait and hope for the best.'

'Okay. See you in the morning.' Falconi drew off by himself to settle in for some serious thinking.

Lieutenant Colonel Winston Baldwin was a liability. And so was Doctor Yoon, the North Korean interrogator. The fight to take both of them across the river would be time consuming and dangerous for everyone. Therefore, only one could go. The Falcon had one hell of a choice to make: who did he allow to live – in other words, which one did he kill – the North Korean or the American jet pilot?'

The former would be an invaluable prisoner. Turned over to the Agency or the boys in one of the MI Detachments assigned to Special Forces, a great deal of useful information could be wrung out of the ancient son of a bitch. Yoon, under the right stimulus, would provide intelligence that had the potential of being applicable and beneficial to the U.S. and its allies for years – perhaps generations – to come.

Then there was Lieutenant Colonel Winston Baldwin, USAF. He was a native American who now loyally served in his third conflict for the United States. He had an impressive aerial combat record which included flying P-38 and P-51 fighter planes against the *Luftwaffe* in World War II. Afterwards, he had qualified for the program to re-train piston-engine pilots for the new jets. A scant five years later, he was back in action. This time as a jet fighter pilot in Korea. He had downed seven MiGs in that conflict to make him an ace in both wars. And, once again, the crack pilot hit the blue for his country in this enigmatic confrontation in Southeast Asia. This time he'd been shot down and captured. It had been vital to get him out of enemy hands to prevent his divulging of vital information to the Communist enemy. That phase of the operation had been completed. Even if he didn't get back to friendly lines, the mission could be chalked up as accomplished.

It was a hell of a thing for a man, after years of unselfish and devoted performance of duties, to face being killed by his own side.

But one of them had to die. Yoon or Baldwin, which one? Falconi's logical side spoke out calmly and coldly, telling him to choose Baldwin. The pilot would have probably made that decision for Falconi if the situation were reversed.

But the Falconi's heart screamed out to him too. It made no demands, yet asked probing, painful questions:

How could he cold-bloodedly murder a fellow American officer?

How could he take a man who'd been a POW and rescue him from the hands of the enemy only to kill him?

What would he say if he were ever to meet the man's family?

He lay back on his poncho and forced his eyes closed. *Shit*, he told himself, *nobody ever said this fucking job would be easy*.

The Soviet helicopter hovered less than fifteen feet above the ground. The soldiers inside, the AK-47's and bandoleers of ammo their only gear, dropped the ropes out the door. They quickly grabbed the dangling lines and shinnied down to the ground displaying wide, satisfied grins.

Lieutenant Phung was so happy he clapped his hands. It was only ten o'clock in the morning, and the scant three hours they had been practicing to exit the aircraft by rope had produced more than a hundred soldiers with enough skill at it to take part in operations.

Those that failed were either naturally clumsy or frightened by even this short height. Phung had to admit that perhaps a dozen or so would be useless in this type of activity, but the speed in which the majority were picking it up more than overcame any disappointment.

Major Dai Vo, the battalion commander, was also pleased, but for a variety of other reasons. This unexpected saving of time and energy meant that his command would be back on active operations that very afternoon. That sly bastard Commissar Hieu would not be able to fault him now. Particularly since he had jumped ahead of schedule in tracking down the imperialists.

Even at that moment, two of the helicopters were out scouting the jungle looking for the fleeing American gangsters.

Choosing the strongest swimmer had been easy. With Lieutenant Bill Thompson of the SEAL as a member of the mission, he had been the logical choice. Any man who had qualified for that group and not only successfully completed their training, but had served a couple of years with them, probably swam by unconscious reflex rather than concentrated effort.

But the Falcon had an additional reason for tasking the navy man with swimming across the difficult river to anchor the rope on the other side. He wanted to get the doctor away from Baldwin. Thompson was forming a growing attachment and affection for the air force officer from caring for him. Falcon had made his decision on which one – Yoon or Baldwin – was to die.

And the choice had been cold and logical.

The Falcon hadn't slept well the night before. As he walked the short distance to the woods where Baldwin had been bedded down, he'd hoped the pilot, at least, had enjoyed this one last night in deep slumber. Lord knows he probably hadn't gotten much in Garrison Three. Falconi stepped into the small clearing where Thompson said he'd stashed the former POW.

He was gone.

Falconi looked around and saw where the air force officer had broken the vegetation walking out of the clearing. At least he had headed for the river where the others were. There would be no need in wasting time hunting him down in the surrounding jungle.

Falcon saw Baldwin standing in the rear of the activities with his back to him. The leader of the Black Eagles pulled the special packet of capsules from his pocket and approached the colonel. At this point it seemed best to have him take the thing then and there with nobody watching. When he keeled over, the men would assume his heart had played out, or the Reds had done something that finally killed him.

Falconi took the pilot by the shoulder and turned him. 'I got something for you to take,' he said softly.

'What is it?' Baldwin asked. His eyes were alert and his face, formerly empty of expression, showed awareness and understanding. 'Bill Thompson already gave me something earlier when I woke up. Are you Captain Falconi?'

'Uh . . . yeah,' the Falcon answered puzzled. 'How're you feeling?'

'Pretty good,' Baldwin said. 'I must admit I'm still fuzzy as hell about what's been going on, but Bill brought me up to date a bit before he went swimming.'

'You know where you are?'

Baldwin smiled. 'I can better describe where I'm not . . . my last real recollection is standing in front of that bastard there.' He pointed to Yoon on the stretcher. 'The guy was putting me through the mill.'

'Jesus!' Falconi exclaimed slipping the brown packet back into his pocket.

'What was that you wanted me to take?'

'Forget it . . . uh, I guess Bill already took care of you', Falcon said lamely. A wild hope for Baldwin's recovery raced through his mind. The best way to find out would be to engage him in conversation. Falconi took a deep breath and crossed his arms. 'You look a hell of a lot better today than yesterday.'

'I suppose I do. I wish I knew what was going on for sure,' Baldwin said.

'Well, I can bring you up to date a bit,' Falconi said taking the pilot by the arm. 'Let's sit over here and chat while the boys hit the river.' They walked to the base of a large tree and settled down. 'Feel like a swim?'

Baldwin smiled broadly. 'I'm really looking forward to it.'

Falcon leaned back and closed his eyes. 'Colonel Baldwin, you'll never know how glad I am to hear you say that.'

Senior Lieutenant Vlademir Krochenko, strapped in the co-pilot's seat of the MI-4 helicopter, peered out the window at the dense greenness of the jungle that flowed slowly beneath the lumbering aircraft.

Next to him, the North Vietnamese pilot demonstrated a lack of finesse in handling the throttle as the chopper's speed fluctuated between forty to fifty knots. But Krochenko was still able to keep up an effective visual sweep of the terrain below.

So far the patrol had been a boring routine of criss-cross patterns trying to pick up some sign of the Americans who had pulled the attack on Garrison Three. Even in the thickest vegetation, it would take the Americans a great deal of skill to avoid detection over a long period of time. Despite the obvious expertise and professionalism of the raiders, the odds were stacked against them. One of the group would eventually betray their outfit. Perhaps the reflection off a carelessly exposed piece of metal equipment, or an upturned face that would stand out against the dark background of the tropical forest would tip off an aerial observer of their location.

Krochenko pointed ahead and spoke to his Oriental counterpart through the intercom. 'Is that cut in the jungle ahead a river?'

'Yes, Comrade Lieutenant,' the pilot answered. 'It is the Mau Xanh.'

The Russian pulled his map from the large pocket on the front of his flight uniform and consulted it. 'Ah, yes! I see.' An easily identifiable bend in the tributary came into view making it easy for him to pinpoint their exact location. 'Then let us fly up and down the river. Perhaps we can spot something along the bank – footprints or something.'

'Yes, Comrade Lieutenant.'

Krochenko's alert eyes scanned the stream for a full five minutes. Then something in the water caught his attention. 'Continue forward for another minute or so, then slowly turn back,' he instructed the pilot.

'Did you spot something, Comrade Lieutenant?'

'Yes. But if there's someone down there, I don't want to make them suspicious,' Krochenko said. He grinned. 'It is easier to see things in water from the air than from the ground, Comrade Pilot. Make a note of that. That is why anti-submarine aircraft always are more effective than surface ships.'

'I will remember that, Comrade Lieutenant,' the pilot said. He eased back the cyclic control to a neutral position to go into a hover. Then he pushed a right rudder and the helicopter spun on its invisible axis to face in the opposite direction. Too much foot pressure caused the tail to continue moving, forcing the pilot to apply opposite rudder to compensate for his sloppy handling of the aircraft.

Krochenko was displeased. 'You must practice your turns, Comrade Pilot. Too much skidding wastes time and effort.'

'Yes, Comrade Lieutenant,' the Vietnamese pilot said embarrassed. He pushed forward on the cyclic and twisted the throttle inboard to cut the rpm. A slower speed would help the Russian check whatever it was he had spotted.

Krochenko's eyes were trained on the water below. An expert observer, he avoided staring fixedly, blinking his eyes constantly and letting them flick back and forth from one side of the river to the other to avoid any undue blurring of his vision. Suddenly he grinned. 'Yes! A rope stretched from one bank to the other, just below the surface.' Suddenly he laughed. 'Yes! Yes! And a naked man just rolled back into the jungle.'

That sighting and the rope was a sure sign of a river crossing operation.

'It's them!' He grabbed the microphone from its place on the instrument panel and quickly transmitted the call sign for the Phu Tong village command post.

Archie Dobbs walked back to the river bank after the chopper continued on its way. 'I hope that sonofabitch didn't spot me,' he said to Dutch Hosteins who joined him. 'That fucking snaplink was jammed on the rope and couldn't get it to open for a couple of seconds. I was caught like a fucking fish on a line.'

'Maybe we'll have luck,' Hosteins said.

'I sure as hell hope so,' Archie said. 'We still got a half dozen guys and that old coot to get across yet.' He signaled back into the trees. Malpractice McCorkel and Lieutenant Bill Thompson, with Doctor Yoon on the litter between them, trotted down to the water.

'We better get this guy over now,' Malpractice said. 'That chopper might be back any minute.'

'Okay,' Dobbs said in agreement. 'Me and Dutch'll help you.' The two scouts, both nude, had been back and forth from one bank to the other at least a half dozen times during the crossing operation. Each took one of the poles of the litter and entered the water. The army medic and navy doctor followed, their burden precariously balanced between them as they slowly edged toward the other side.

Lightfingers O'Quinn and Horny Galchaser, also bare-assed naked on the opposite bank, slipped into the river and fought the strong current until they reached the others. They took positions on the middle part of the litter, and now all six men fought to keep the North Korean interrogator, unconscious and unaware of what was going on, from being pitched into the water.

'I hope this ancient fart appreciates our efforts,' Galchaser said.

'Well, if he don't you can console yourself with the thought that MI and the CIA will,' O'Quinn said.

The six men continued the struggle until finally, Archie and Hosteins made contact with the river bank. Other willing hands appeared and Doctor Yoon Hwan was safely delivered to the other side.

Falconi hadn't stripped for his own crossing. Now the heavy humidity prevented his uniform from drying out despite the fact he'd been out of the water for over an hour. He joined his men. 'Let's shake it up, guys,' he urged them. 'If that chopper spotted anything, we'll be in deep shit mighty quick.'

'Yeah,' Archie Dobbs said surveying the high cliffs that pinned them to the river. 'And between the rock and the hard place too.'

FIFTEEN

Emitting an unperceivable battle cry, Lieutenant Phung Xuan grasped the rope and swung out of the helicopter and rapidly descended through the trees to the ground below. Within moments he was joined by his radio operator. The other men of his attack force were soon assembled beneath the hovering aircraft.

Each man had only the barest fighting essentials on his body. An AK-47 assault rifle, two bandoleers of ammo, and a canteen were all that made up the combat load. They had even left their pith helmets behind, as they moved rapidly through the jungle toward their objective.

Across the river, on the high bluffs looking down on the banks of the Mau Xanh, a similar group rappeled to the ground. This was the ambush force, which would keep the Americans pinned between the river and the bluff, thus preventing them from being able to escape to the cover of the deep forest.

Tung ho! The imperialists were at last trapped. And there were MiG-17s now orbiting not far away waiting to be called in on fire support to blast the interlopers into surrender. And, to make things easier, higher headquarters in Hanoi had decided to sacrifice both Colonel Nguyen Chi Roi and the North Korean Doctor Yoon in this effort to annihilate the attack group. Even the government in P'yong Yang concurred that it was best to let Yoon die than risk his being taken farther south.

Phung called his commo man over and took the receiver-transmitter of the radio. He pressed the transmission lever and spoke into it. 'Lead Aircraft, this is Ground Control over.'

The answer was immediate. 'Ground Control, Lead Aircraft, over.'

Phung could scarcely contain the excitement in his voice. 'This is Ground Control. Stand by. Contact with enemy is imminent. Over.'

The jet pilot, as anxious as the Infantry officer to get into the fight, answered, 'Affirmative, Ground Control. Attack aircraft are prepared for full commitment.'

'Shit!'

Falconi's voice sounded even over the noise of the choppers hovering over the bluffs above them.

'There's others on the opposite side, Skipper,' Dobbs informed him.

'Yeah. I know,' the Falcon said. 'We couldn't get across the river again anyhow, but those bastards above have blocked us in down here.'

'Hell, sir, we've been able to fight through 'em anyhow,' Dobbs said, not feeling discouraged. 'What's to stop us now?'

'Nothing's to stop us,' Falconi said. 'But this is going to be real hairy. And we're going to have to move slow and sure or we'll just keep walking into ambushes until we're cut down to zilch.'

Both stopped talking as the motors of the helicopters suddenly faded away when the aircraft swung up and out of the area of operations.

'There they go,' Dobbs said. 'They've left the ground troops behind. Me and Dutch had better have a look and spot their positions before you make any plans, Skipper.'

'Right. You have paper for a sketch map?'

'Yeah, Skipper,' Dobbs said. The sergeant was an excellent illustrator, and his eye for detail and proper perspective made him invaluable in quick drawings of battlefield situations. 'We oughta be back in an hour.'

'Make it faster if –' Falconi stopped talking.

'What's the matter, Skipper?'

'Shhh!' The Falcon listened intently. Then he grimaced. 'Goddamnit it!'

Archie Dobbs had heard it too. 'Jets!'

'If those bastards have an air support, we're really in a world of serious trouble,' Falconi said. 'You and Dutch had better move damned fast. And send the Top and Ritchie to me on your way out.'

'Right, Skipper.' The two scouts disappeared into the undergrowth.

In moments, the two leaders of the mission's fire teams were squatting with their commander. The Falcon wasted no time. 'Top, you'll watch the river.' He turned to Lieutenant Ritchie Wakely. 'Loan him a couple of your guys, then put the rest out to cover Archie and Dutch. When they get back they may have an NVA regiment on their asses.'

By then the jets had reached the operational area.

Phung's men were spread along the riverbank. Thirty muzzles of AK47s pointed toward the American positions. On the company commander's orders, they cut loose, the 7.62 millimeter slugs zapping into the vegetation on the other side like hundreds of angry hornets.

'Lead Aircraft, this is Ground Control, over,' Phung said over the roar of the weaponry.

'This is Lead Aircraft, over.'

'The target is on the south bank of the river, between the bend on the north and the declining elevation toward the south, over,' Phung said.

'Do you mean in front of the bluffs, over?' the pilot asked.

'Affirmative, comrade,' Phung sang out. 'They are between those cliffs and the river there.'

'An easy target. *Tren dich de ban!* Our attack is commencing!'

The Black Eagles dove for cover as the forest around them exploded under the impact of the KPV machine guns' 14.5 millimeter slugs.

Lieutenant Dinky Dow, with his two prisoners and guard detail, had withdrawn off into a depression that was relatively safe in the hail of screeching metal.

The attack broke off and the thundering roar of the jets disappeared into the blazing sky. Several of the men coughed in the dust kicked up by the incoming bullets. Broken leaves and vegetation continued to flutter down on top of them for a couple of minutes.

'Casualties?' Falconi called out. He was pleased to have no reports. 'Hang in there. They'll hit us again and we won't be able to get outta here 'til Archie and Dutch get back.'

'Air attack!' someone called out by the book as the growing noise of the jets again descended on them.

The jungle splattered and roared with the attack. Demond Carter, over in Bravo Fire Team, seemed to leap straight up in the air, then collapse to the ground.

When the assault broke off, Malpractice McCorkel rushed to the downed sergeant. A quick examination was all that it took. 'He's had it, Falcon,' Malpractice called in answer to the unasked question.

'You guys stay in close to the ground,' Falconi yelled out wishing each man had brought an entrenching tool with him. Contingency plans are great, but when they mean an extra load to carry in dense tropical forest, it's best to go without them. And, anyway, whose imagination would have been perceptive enough to know they would be required to dig in on a rescue mission?

'They're coming back!'

The first aircraft rent the air with its machine guns, and once more their confined world exploded under the impact of the slugs. But a newer, deadlier element now entered the game when the napalm bomb hit at the water's edge and threw its fiery hell straight ahead.

SFC Manuel Rivera, screamed his agony, and scrambled to his feet to run in a fiery frenzy, his entire body enveloped in the flames. He reached the river bank where the NVA, in unintentional mercy, cut him down with the AK47s.

Archie Dobbs and Dutch Hosteins, back from patrol, took advantage of the short lull to rush through the area and dive to the ground beside Falconi. The captain looked at his scout team, the concern evident in his expression. 'What's up on those bluffs?'

'Bad news, Skipper,' Dobbs said. 'We're ringed in real tight. There ain't no way we can bust through the bastards. Some more choppers came in behind the air strikes and they got reinforcements behind the fucking reinforcements.'

Falconi looked at Hosteins. 'What would the Foreign Legion do in a situation like this?'

'Give their lives for France, *mon capitaine*,' he answered.

'The United States Army has discouraged preconceived last stands since Custer's fiasco,' Falconi said. 'Did you make that sketch map, Archie?'

'Right, Skipper,' Dobbs said handing it over. 'And, believe me, things look worse even on paper.'

Falconi studied the drawing for several minutes. 'Jesus Christ! There's fifteen of us left. Even if we split up and take off individually, only two or three could make it.'

'With luck,' Archie Dobbs added.

'Yeah,' Falconi said.

Suddenly the air reverberated with the approaching roar of jets.

'Air attack!'

The men hugged the ground, some even squirming in an effort to sink lower into the protective earth while their world exploded and bucked under the Soviet aircraft machine guns. This time the napalm came in too high and splattered into the bluffs above them. The burning jelly streaked out ominously, but harmlessly into unoccupied jungle.

'We gotta do something fast, Skipper,' Archie Dobbs said. 'There ain't too much –' He stopped speaking and looked at Hosteins beside him. 'Hey, Dutch? You Okay?' He rolled his friend over. 'Oh, shit, Dutch!'

The German's face was blanched and pinched in agony. The wound indicated a shoulder entry and a massive exit by the kidneys. '*Je suis verwunder* – I'm hit.'

Falconi motioned for Lieutenant Thompson to crawl over to them. 'Dutch is hit, Bill,' he called out.

'Tell him . . . to stay . . . where he is,' Hosteins said with labored breathing. He was a man who had been in constant combat from 1939 until 1956. He had seen enough wounds in those seventeen years to be able to recognize the seriousness of his own. He looked around at the tropical vegetation above him. 'I suppose . . . I was never meant to . . . leave here . . . *nich wahr?*'

Falconi looked at the dying legionnaire. His escape from Dien Bien Phu had been blind luck when fate was looking the other way. The Falcon had learned of *karma* in his martial arts training. A man's destiny was pre-ordained and he could do nothing to alter it. Hosteins was meant to die in the green hell of Indo-China, and his life since then had slowly evolved to bring him back there for just that purpose.

The gods of War had never wanted Bruno Hosteins to leave the Foreign Legion. They wanted him to report in to Valhalla wearing the *kepi blanc*, and this was Odin and Thor's way of putting things right.

'Hang in there, Dutch,' Archie Dobbs said. 'You gotta go live with your brother in New Jersey. You're needed on that farm, man. Just grit your teeth and we'll get you the hell back to the real world.'

But Dutch's vision was already clouding over. His dilating pupils could now see beyond the world in which Falconi and the Black Eagles lived. He perceived shadowy shapes approaching him. Within moments Hosteins could make out they were men – men wearing the leopard pattern of the Legion *paras*. Men who had given up the ghost in this same jungle in the final spasms of France's effort to maintain her Indo-Chinese colonial possessions. The phantoms looked down at *Sergent* Bruno Hosteins and called out the battle cry to him in a silent, hollow ring:

'*A moi la Légion!*'

Lieutenant Phung Xuan put the binoculars to his eyes and trained them on the still smoldering corpse of the American. Blackened and twisted by the flames that had consumed it, the cadaver lay in full view on the river bank.

The NVA officer's lips twisted into a wry smile. It was only a matter of time before any living thing between the bluffs and the water would be pounded or burned into mangled charcoal.

'Lead Aircraft,' he spoke into the microphone. 'You are on target. Continue the attack, over.'

'Affirmative, Ground Control,' the pilot replied.

Phung watched the MiGs come in over the tree line, their machine guns blazing, sending tracer shells streaking into the enemy positions opposite him.

The second airplane came in and released the napalm cannister. Phung watched the object sail toward him, sinking lower as it streaked along its trajectory. It kept dropping, dropping, dropping. His eyes widened.

'Get down! *An tranh!*' he screamed at his men.

The bomb passed so close overhead, the young officer could hear its whistling sound. It hit the far bank just at the river line, sending the burning jelly bouncing high into the air and back toward the NVA positions. Three of his men ran screaming, completely covered in flames, to fling themselves into the cooling waters of the Mau Xahn in futile efforts to save themselves.

'Lead Aircraft! Lead Aircraft!' Phung screamed into the microphone. 'Tell your wingman to use more skill with the napalm! He almost scored a direct hit on us! Three of my men have now died for socialism!'

The pilot's voice crackled over the air. 'We regret the inaccuracy, Comrade. But we are not yet used to bombsights on our aircraft. They are electronic and respond badly if the setting is not locked in properly. Over.'

Phung, not ignorant of his countryman's difficulty with advanced technology, spoke with panic in his voice. 'Lead Aircraft, continue attack with machine guns. Do not, I say again, *do not* use napalm unless I specifically call for it! Over!'

'Affirmative, Ground Control. Will that suffice under these conditions? Over.'

'Yes! The heavy automatic weaponry is tearing them up. It is easy for us to see from here. Attack! Attack!'

The incoming 14.5 millimeter slugs whistled and slapped into the vegetation. Lieutenant Colonel Winston Baldwin ducked as twigs and other vegetable debris peppered his face. He was not impressed with the North Vietnamese pilots' performance. And Baldwin knew well that they most assuredly were not Russian. The napalm hits up on the bluff and down by the river were inexcusable.

But the confines of the space they were in did not call for a high degree of accuracy to be effective. Although the USAF pilot was not well trained in ground combat, it was obvious to him that their situation could hardly be worse. There was a river in front of them, that could only be crossed carefully and slowly under the best of conditions. And behind were high bluffs that would call for the same amount of careful consideration – even if there weren't NVA infantry dug in there.

Baldwin began to appreciate the groundpounder's position in war now. Despite combat flying in two conflicts, he had never had the opportunity to know how physically uncomfortable ground fighting really was. He'd always had a full belly and good living quarters to return to after engaging in the impersonal and rather detached work of dogfights or ground support. Right now, he knew, even the North Vietnamese pilots were incapable of relating to or appreciating the hell of being under aerial attack by modern weapons.

Now, more than ever, Baldwin wanted to get back in a jet fighter and turn it loose on some NVA sons of bitches – particularly the little bastards on the other side of the river.

Not far from him, Lieutenant Dinky Dow turned the prisoners over to Sergeants Marvin Dayton and Ray Limo. He took advantage of the short lull between air attacks to rush through their positions and slam himself to the earth beside Robert Falconi.

'Hey, Falcon,' he said. 'How long we last through this shit? We lucky and got no casualties for awhile. But that change pretty fucking *mau le*.'

'Got any ideas, Dinky Dow?' Falconi asked almost with sarcasm.

'I can't do much here, Falcon,' the ex-Viet Cong said. 'But maybe if I cross river, maybe something happen that would help us.'

Falconi gave the matter some quick, but considerate, thought. Dinky Dow's talents were a thousandfold and deadly when it came to sneaking-and-peeking. If there was anything at all possible that could be done, he would do it. The Falcon nodded. 'You got my permission to go over there and look around. But it's gonna be mighty hairy, Dinky Dow.'

'What you think it is here, Falcon?' the Vietnamese asked with a sardonic grin. 'And, anyhow, what difference it make which side of Mau Xanh I die on?'

SIXTEEN

It would have been impossible for three or more men to have crossed the Mau Xanh River at that point on that particular day. Even for only two men it would have been improbable.

One man did do it.

Diminutive Lieutenant Nguyen Van Dow – Dinky Dow to his fellow members of the Black Eagles – took his time by moving slowly through jungle with the patience of a stalking jaguar coupled with long periods of immobility that would have taxed a serpent. The wily Vietnamese, with a natural, untutored knowledge of human psychology, would wait until the three MiGs came thundering in for an attack. He knew that all eyes would be on the aircraft, and that was the best time to make his moves. It took him almost three hours before he had emerged dripping on the opposite side of the river. There the main element of the North Vietnamese 327th Infantry Battalion waited for the representatives of the Red air force to continue pounding the space where the Americans and their prisoners had been driven.

Dinky Dow crawled two hundred meters straight into the brush before he turned toward the enemy positions. Again, this was extra effort on his part – but it paid off. He didn't stumble across any observation posts, nor was he discovered by wandering NVA soldiers.

Dinky Dow's superb talent as a jungle fighter wasn't all instinctive. He had once been a dedicated Viet Cong and was given the complete course in the furtive, clandestine combat that was their specialty. This was further enhanced by practical battle experience where failure was marked by death. Through a small amount of luck and a large amount of developing expertise, the five-foot, three inch tall dynamo soon earned a place among the very best of the VC's fighting elite. He used his short stature to advantage, staying low and out of sight. His light weight made his tread naturally soft and silent, whether it be on spongy jungle terrain or across the gravel parade ground of an infiltrated garrison.

He noticed that the aircraft had not returned. They would be on their way back to their base for refueling and to restock their ammunition. A plan had formed in Dinky Dow's mind, and it involved the use of those MiGs. And the feisty little guy had the audacity to want them fully re-armed and gassed.

Movement became easier for him because the NVA soldiers had taken up the slack left by the departed aircraft. They laid down a murderous fusillade into the Black Eagles' area with their assault rifles, the constant firing creating a near unending din. Dinky Dow also realized this would be safer for the Americans, since it was necessary for the Reds to fire up at the higher river bank on the other side. The angle of their shooting was so steep it missed a large portion of the target area.

The Vietnamese officer still moved carefully, but his speed was much greater than before. The unending bursts of fire from the NVA positions pinpointed the areas of danger and he was able to avoid them. He made a calculated guess as to where his objective might be. As he penetrated deeper into the NVA unit, he once again had to slow down. Dinky Dow now listened for voices giving orders. Then each one would have to be checked out until he found the one unknown individual he was looking for.

The first was a sergeant changing the position of a careless soldier who had gotten himself situated into a spot with a limited field of fire. Dinky Dow grinned at the anger in the NCO's voice, then continued his patient search.

The NVA troops cut loose with some more fusillades directed at the opposite river bank.

The next place was a squad leader arranging for the men who wished to relieve themselves to do so in turn. This caught the infiltrator among several troops moving back and forth. Dinky Dow, forced to squeeze himself beneath a palm, froze motionless while a soldier urinated only a meter's distance. The warm liquid splattered in his face. Three more Reds tended to their need before Dinky Dow was able to wipe off the piss and continue his silent, deadly quest.

More volleys kept bursting out at regular intervals as the NVA unit kept the pressure on the Americans they had trapped between the river and the bluffs.

Another voice which attracted his attention turned out to be a corporal issuing ammunition to representatives from various squads. Even Dinky Dow was getting discouraged now and he had almost made up his mind to go back through the unit to see if he'd missed what he was looking for, when he saw it.

The end of a whip antenna.

The uninvited guest moved back deeper in the jungle and made a wide circle to come up behind his objective. When he finally reached his desired position, he took a careful look around to note the actual situation he had moved into.

There were two men in a small clearing. One, obviously a commo man, sat near the radio that he carried around for the other. The officer was a lieutenant, and he held the transmitter-receiver in his hand as if waiting.

Finally he spoke, 'Lead Aircraft, this is Ground Control. Over. Lead Aircraft, this is Ground Control Over.'

There was evidently no response on the radio. But at least Dinky Dow now knew the call signs used on the air strikes.

The young soldier looked up at the officer. 'How long will they be gone, Comrade Lieutenant?'

'I expect them back at any moment,' the officer said.

Dinky Dow moved in.

'Lead Aircraft, this is Ground Control. Over.'

The infiltrator, his knife pulled, reached the edge of the clearing. One more step would put him right behind the soldier squatting there.

Dinky Dow waited for another long burst of gunfire to squelch the sound of a scream. Then the ex-VC's knife sliced into the young radio operator's back.

Lieutenant Phung Xuan whirled at the movement he caught out of the corner of his eye in time to see the commo man die, blood spurting from between his lips. The attacker pivoted on his left foot, the right one catching the NVA lieutenant in the solar plexus in an explosive thrust kick. The Red's diaphragm froze, cutting off all breathing an instant before Dinky Dow's panther punch smashed his adam's apple ending a promisary military career for the ambitious young officer.

The firing continued at the unseen targets across the river.

'Keep your heads down and watch for ricochets,' Falconi shouted in the clearing.

Archie Dobbs, still sweating heavily after burying Hosteins, sat behind a thick tree enjoying a sip of lukewarm water from his canteen. 'What do you figure Dinky Dow is up to, Skipper?'

The Falcon shrugged. 'I don't know. It was a long shot that he could accomplish anything.'

'Them planes oughta be back anytime,' Dobbs said. 'Won't take 'em long to refuel and reload their shooting irons.'

'We'll make our move when they do,' Falconi said. 'There's no sense in sitting here waiting to be napalmed. Fetch Ritchie and Top for me.'

'You bet, Skipper.' Dobbs put his canteen away and crawled off beneath the high angled shots coming their way to tend to the errand.

The two team leaders showed the strain as they joined their commanding officer. Ritchie tried to grin, but his eyes weren't getting with his program of jocularity.

Snow, ever the top sergeant, settled in looking business-like.

'I'll make it short and sweet,' Falconi said. 'We've had the weinie.'

The two said nothing, only accepting the fact stoically while waiting for orders.

'Dinky Dow's across the river,' the Falcon said. 'I don't have much hope there. It was worth an effort though. When the aircraft return, I'm going to eliminate the prisoners. A unit our size can't make it back, but individuals can. The air attack will make the NVA duck, particularly since they might catch some of it too, so that'll be the best time for us to bug out o' here. We'll split up in no more than two-man teams and take our chances.'

'We'll be lucky if even one of those pairs make it,' Master Sergeant Snow said calmly.

'Who knows? With luck . . .' Falconi let the statement hang. 'It's not fancy, but it's all we got. Brief your men and wait for my orders.' He reached out and shook their hands. 'Good luck, guys. And pass that on to the others, okay?'

'Yes, sir,' Snow said.

Falconi watched them crawl past Dobbs. Archie winked at

him. 'What about you and me, Skipper? Want to buddy up?'

'Sure. Why not?' Falconi checked his M16. 'And while you're steppin'-and-fetchin', get me Thompson.'

Wordlessly, Dobbs went off again. When Thompson reported in, he was not happy. The SEAL got straight to the point. 'I already got the word. We're withdrawing in ones and twos, huh? Okay, I'll take Baldwin with me.'

'You know Baldwin's not trained for this kind of stuff,' Falconi said. 'And you also know what has to be done about the situation, right?'

'Give me the orders precisely,' Thompson insisted.

'I'll take care of it,' Falconi said. 'Just get him over here. I'll give him one of these.' He pulled the special brown packet from his pocket.

'I figured you had something like that,' Thompson said looking at the cyanide. 'But don't you think Baldwin will wonder why you're giving him medicine and I'm not?' He reached out and took the deadly poison. 'But I want you to give me verbal orders . . . *sir*.'

'Okay, Bill. You are to kill Colonel Baldwin. I'm making it a direct order,' Falconi said. 'Is that clear enough for you? We can't let him fall back into their hands under any circumstances.'

'Yes, sir.'

Falconi, his heart breaking, motioned Thompson to leave. He looked up at Archie Dobbs who had stumbled back onto the scene. 'Well, goddamn it! What the hell else can I do?'

'Nothing, Skipper. What about the two prisoners? Want me to handle that for you?'

'No,' Falconi answered. 'I'll do it myself. And I want you to be quiet about this – now and forever!'

'You call, I haul . . .' Dobbs let the statement hang unfinished.

The sound of jet aircraft sounded in the distance.

'Let's get ready,' Falconi said.

The noise grew until it became a roar. Then the undeniable sound of rocket fire erupted.

'Boy!' Dobbs exclaimed. 'When those fuckers reload, they don't mess around, huh?'

They hit the ground. But the explosions were on the bluffs above them.

'Ha!' Dobbs crowed. 'The dumb bastards hit their own positions.'

Falconi grinned back. 'Then let's enjoy it until they find our range again, huh? There's no sense in trying to reach the top of the bluffs until the air strike stops pounding there.'

The next attack was the same. But this time there was napalm and machine gun fire added to the din.

'A coupla more runs like that and the mother-fuckers will have it all cleared away for us up there,' Falconi mused.

There, indeed, were two more attacks that hit the NVA positions above the Black Eagles – then several more.

'Shit!' Archie Dobbs yelled in glee. 'It's almost as if someone's directing them back there.'

'Yeah . . .' Then Falconi yelled loudly. 'Dinky Dow! The little fucker's got to their radio. He's calling in air strikes on their positions behind us. We can . . . oh, shit! Thompson and Baldwin.' He leaped to his feet and tore through the underbrush until he reached the two.

Baldwin was laughing. 'The incompetent asses are blowing our way the hell out of here, aren't they?'

'They sure are, Colonel,' Falconi said. He looked at Thompson. 'You didn't . . .'

'Hell, no,' the SEAL said.

'What's going on?' Baldwin asked.

'Nothing, Colonel, except we're getting out of here as a complete unit as soon as those air strikes break off. By the way, we're not being treated to a demonstration of North Vietnamese pilot error. Our guy Dinky Dow made it to the other side of the river. He's calling the bastards in to zap the bastards up on those bluffs for us.'

Falconi turned and started to shout for Archie Dobbs, but the sergeant was standing behind him grinning. 'Okay, Skipper, I know. You wanna see Ritchie and Top again right?'

'You bet your sweet ass,' Falcon said laughing.

Dinky Dow thanked whatever poverty or piss-poor planning there was that had given the commandment regarding the dearth of commo gear in NVA infantry battalions. Had there been another radio with the unit on the bluff, they would have immediately notified the two smug MiG pilots that they were rocketing, napalming and machine gunning their own troops.

Now that the aircraft were again low on fuel and munitions, they had knocked off for the day, expecting the attack to continue on the ground. And, for Dinky Dow, it was time to take his leave as guest commander of the 327th Infantry Battalion's forward elements.

He kicked the Russian radio over and jumped up letting his 115 pound body land on it. Once, twice, thrice more and the instrument was smashed, making all effective communications for this portion of NVA over and done with.

With no orders to cease firing, the troops along the river bank kept shooting across the water. The initial enthusiasm had waned somewhat, however, and the rate of fire had dropped off.

Dinky Dow turned to melt back into the jungle, but an NVA sergeant – who had finally gone to the CP to find out when they were going to cross the river – blundered into the clearing. The NCO tried desperately to unsling his AK47, but the ARVN lieutenant's M16 barked first. The rounds smacked into the bandoleer around the Red's body driving extra bits of metal into his flesh. Knocked to his ass, he took another 5.56 millimeter round full in the face to end his days of service to Uncle Ho.

Shouts from nearby indicated the shots had been heard by others, and they knew something was definitely not *chura* at the command post. Dinky Dow, forced to go in the opposite direction, melted into the jungle at the same time a corporal and two privates charged into the clearing from the other side.

Russian bullets spat and whined in ricochet around the short ex-VC. He turned to face them, dropping to his knees while, at the same time, pulling a grenade from his patrol harness. The pin was yanked, and a skinny arm sent the explosive device sailing through the tall leaves of the jungle plants.

Screams followed the explosion. Dinky Dow emptied the remaining rounds of his magazine in the same direction, then jumped up and raced away.

His next plan of action was to get back across the river and link back up with the Black Eagles. And, aware his comrades would now be scaling the bluffs above what had once seemed the scene of their last stand, the fiesty Vietnamese knew he was going to have some difficult times ahead of him.

* * *

Archie Dobbs climbed over the top of the bluff and dropped to all fours. He could hear a few moans but no other sign of active life around him. Moving forward a few yards, he found the first corpse. Burned almost beyond recognition as a human being, the soldier lay in a large charred area of the jungle.

Dobbs ran quick recons in an area some fifty yards in circumference. The NVA unit there, set up to ambush and pin down the Black Eagles, was now beyond any effectiveness. The scout went back to the edge of the bluff and whistled a low signal.

Within a minute Falconi appeared a few feet below. He crawled up to Dobbs. 'How's it look?'

'There's a few wounded, Skipper,' Dobbs reported. 'But the way's clear now.'

'Great.' The Falcon signaled back to Master Sergeant Snow. 'Okay, Top. Let's resume our walk to the south.'

Fire Team Bravo, now consisting of only Snow, Lightfingers O'Quinn and Jan Miskoski were the first on the high ground. They moved on to make room for the others.

Ritchie Wakely, Horny Galchaser and Calvin Culpepper of Fire Team Alpha were the next to appear. They were followed by Ray Limo who immediately turned when he reached the summit of the bluff. He aimed his weapon down and kept a careful eye as Malpractice McCorkel appeared with the front end of the litter bearing Doctor Yoon. Seconds later an angry Colonel Nguyen, on the other end of the stretcher struggled to the top. Ex-POW Marvin Dayton was jabbing the NVA officer in the ass with his M16 to hurry him along.

Finally Lieutenant Bill Thompson and Lieutenant Colonel Winston Baldwin brought up the rear.

Dobbs turned to Falconi. 'What about Dinky Dow?'

'We can't wait for him, Archie.'

'I know,' Archie said. 'The little fucker saved our asses, Skipper. Y'know, I wouldn't mind going back for a look-see.'

'No dice, Archie. We gotta get out of here,' Falconi said.

'How about just squatting down and waiting for him?'

Falconi ignored the request. He nodded toward the south. 'Take the point.'

'Sure, Skipper. Just a thought. How many guys have we lost altogether now?'

'Seven,' Falconi answered. 'Eight if we don't hear from Dinky Dow again.'

'I hate to go off, Skipper,' Dobbs said.

'We can't fuck around here, Archie. Not only will the NVA have people coming across the Mau Xanh after us, but the whole fucking Commie army between here and South Vietnam will have been alerted by now.'

'And us with two POWs to herd along too,' Dobbs added. He looked around then stopped. 'Shit! For a minute I forgot I'd lost Dutch. Won't be the same on point without him.'

'Yeah,' the Falcon said. He wondered if their *karma* would be similar to the ex-legionnaire's. At least he'd been lucky and had gained some extra time before Valhalla's call.

SEVENTEEN

The jungle heat settled down over the detachment like an invisible, smothering blanket of muggy pressure. After the hour's climb to the top of the bluff and another four of unceasing movement, Falconi finally called a halt to give the men the breather they so desperately needed.

And he had to take stock of their situation too.

Now low on rations, ammo and even medical supplies, the mission, carefully planned to last a maximum of twenty-four hours, was well into its third day – with many more to come. The first thing Falconi had to do was re-organize his small force. Counting both Colonel Baldwin and Sergeant Dayton as members of the unit now – and considering Dinky Dow as lost – they had sustained 38% casualties.

The two prisoners, Colonel Nguyen and Doctor Yoon, were also another consideration that Falconi had to contend with. Nguyen was in excellent physical condition, but the old North Korean was damned near comatose. That had to be dealt with too. But first he had to re-organize.

The new set-up was arranged under the KISS principle: Keep It Simple, Stupid.

COMMAND

CPT FALCONI, Robert

RECON ELEMENT

SSG DOBBS, Archie
SGT LIMO, Ray

FIRE TEAM ALPHA

ILT WAKELY, Ritchie, Team Leader
SFC GALCHASER, Jack
SGT CULPEPPER, Calvin

PRISONER DETAIL

LT THOMPSON, Bill
SFC MC CORKEL, Malcomb
SSG DAYTON, Marvin
LCL BALDWIN, Winston

FIRE TEAM BRAVO

MSG SNOW, John
SFC MISKOSKI, Jan
SSG O'QUINN, Liam

Falconi had taken Sergeant Ray Limo and put him with Archie Dobbs to give the scout the backup fire power he might need in the event of an unexpected withdrawal back to the main body. Combining the medical and guard teams had seemed a natural and expeditious way of giving Thompson something to occupy him besides keeping track of Colonel Baldwin. That way he could also provide security on one of the flanks and relieve Malpractice McCorkel and Dayton in the task of guarding the NVA officer Colonel Nguyen.

The next order of business was the elimination of Doctor Yoon. The old man seemed to be unconscious most of the time and required a litter. Falconi felt he could no longer afford giving the Korean the care required to get the man back south. Besides, carrying the stretcher was exhausting work – even with Nguyen on one end of the thing. Falconi knew that he would need a bushel of Kotex to stuff up his ass after Clayton Andrews of the CIA chewed it bloody for killing the interrogator, but there was really not much of an argument in favor of trying to get the North Korean back. It would be bad enough as it was. At least the west could console itself knowing that Yoon's death would be a severe loss to the Communists in their handling of free world prisoners.

Falconi, as with Baldwin, would follow the strictest procedures. Men involved in the sorts of missions and operations the Black Eagles participated in knew full well that assassinations were not always directed at well-armed, protected opponents. Sometimes the helpless, or even people on one's own side, had to be taken out. But when such procedures were necessary, they were handled discreetly and quietly – even within the confines of a close-knit team.

The less people who knew about a situation, the fewer individuals there are that can inadvertently give away classified information regarding it.

Falconi had sent Archie Dobbs and Ray Limo forward to pull a recon to pick out the best route to follow the rest of that afternoon. Marvin Dayton had taken Colonel Nguyen off to keep him under tight guard. The former prisoner amused himself by keeping the NVA officer busy performing push-ups during the breaks and pauses in the operations.

The rest of the detachment was situated in a wide circle to form a defensive perimeter, waiting for the recon team's return. Falconi had made sure the defense position was spread out enough that the men would need radio contact to regroup. This wasn't only because it would make it difficult for the NVA to pull off any surprise attacks or encounters, but it would also allow most of his men to escape in case the enemy hit them.

And Falcon wanted to make sure no one heard any thrashing that Yoon might perform in his dying throes.

The Falcon stood alone in a grassy space between two groves of heavy palm bushes. Doctor Yoon Hwan lay on a stretcher near the American, his eyes closed tightly and his mouth slightly parted while he breathed in short labored gasps. The elderly man had drifted off into one of his many spells of unconsciousness.

Falconi got the packet of cyanide from his pocket and pulled out a capsule. He glanced down at the prisoner, then turned slowly around to make sure none of the men had come back to see him on some business or other. He sensed the movement behind him. A little angry, he turned to see who had left the perimeter to bullshit with him.

Yoon Hwan was standing erect, his eyes displaying an intensity and concentration that belied his former unconscious state. He said nothing, but his entire being seemed alert and aimed dead on the Falcon.

Falcon snarled. 'What the fuck are you . . .'

Yoon leaped straight up into the air and delivered a flying side-kick at the American's head.

Falconi threw up a clumsy high block with his left arm that resulted in a bad bruise, but at least the death-dealing attack had been thwarted. Yoon moved rapidly off to one side, knowing he had to move fast before the American could summon aid from his men. He exploded into a rapid combination of *Tae Kwondo* punches and kicks.

Falconi countered with a slashing *shuto* chop that caught the old man's shoulder. Yoon, however, went with the force of the blow, hit the ground and rolled neatly to his feet facing his opponent in the T-position.

'You old bastard,' Falconi said not without a hint of admiration in his voice. 'Resting up your ass by fooling us into hauling you around for the past days.'

'The elderly require quiescence,' Yoon said. He tried an iron-broom, sweeping his leg at Falconi's feet to attempt to trip him, but the Falcon was able to leap out of its path.

Again they faced each other. Falconi could tell he was up against a master of *Tae Kwondo* – a Korean form of karate. Despite his advanced years, Yoon was in a physical condition that might be envied by men thirty years younger. This superb achievement accomplished through the spiritual as well as the practical application of martial arts discipline.

Falconi drew back into the horse-stance, but after only two beats of waiting he launched an attack which began with a stamp kick, continued through with a round-house *seiken* punch, a lateral elbow smash, and terminating with a spinning side-kick.

All four efforts missed.

'You are accomplished,' Yoon said despite the failure of the attack. 'But you lack a certain finesse. That great plane of the martial arts can only be accomplished through many years of study and meditation.'

Falcon nodded. 'Of course. The state of attainment which gives a man complete physical and spiritual control over his body requires decades of unselfish devotion.'

'Then the student becomes a master, thus being able to confuse even a skilled physician regarding the true condition of his health,' Yoon added.

'As you did Lieutenant Thompson,' Falcon said.

'I am sure he is an excellent doctor, but he made presumptions based on his western upbringing and education,' Yoon said. 'They are not applicable to –' He laughed wryly. '– old Korean farts.'

'My apologies, Master Doctor Yoon,' Falconi said sincerely. 'Perhaps it would be better if I saved myself further punishment by shooting you.'

'I have been ready to die for many, many years,' Yoon said. 'And I am sure you will do what you think best in this situation.'

Falconi considered a quick-draw of his .45. He knew he could get the pistol out and shoot Yoon before even that expert could close the gap between them. But the noise of such a shot would alert any NVA searchers in the area. And he was sure that, even if they didn't know the detachment's exact location, the Reds were close enough to hear the shot. Another helicopter-borne attack might prove fatal to the Black Eagles.

Falconi would have to take Yoon with his bare hands.

Yoon suddenly came forward and pivoted into a wheel kick, which carried him all the way around to counter against Falconi's forearm parry. The old Korean grabbed the American's wrist and pulled him into a circle throw. Dropping backward to the ground, Yoon's foot rose to meet Falcon's midsection and the older man pumped his leg to send the American hurtling overhead. The maneuver was well calculated. Falconi was unable to come out of it properly, crashing into the thick trunk of a nearby tree in the recovery phase of the movement.

Falconi, stunned, staggered back and was instantly grasped into a forearm vice hold. He could feel the tightening of the grip around his neck. The pressure cut off his breathing and made his neck feel like each separate vertebra was popping and turning in a different direction. He tried to ram an elbow into his opponent's ribs, but failed. Yoon's grip continued to grow stronger . . . deadlier.

Extreme vertigo disoriented Falconi and the lack of oxygen began its insidious encroachment into his brain's ability to think and react. He suddenly shuddered in a display of growing unconsciousness, then slumped into a relaxed, motionless state – for one millisecond.

Suddenly, unexpectedly, the American broke loose and slammed a foot on top of Yoon's, putting all his strength into the attack. Falconi felt the bones give way. A quick, straight punch with his right missed, but he had some small satisfaction in feeling the partial contact of the same thing in his left hand.

Yoon staggered back, threw out both hands in a X-block to avoid Falconi's *shuto* swing, but the American's unexpected snap-kick hit the old man in the center of the abdomen.

Yoon's breath exploded out and he went down, but rolled back and regained his feet. He moved deftly to the litter on which he had been carried such a distance. Grabbing one of the poles he pulled it free and instantly switched his fighting method from *karate* to *bojutsu*.

Now Falcon leaped and whirled to avoid Yoon's slashing, skillful attacks with the pole. By deftly sliding the instrument back and forth, the Korean varied the length of the staff with each movement he made.

Yoon struck with a short *chiheisen no* slash, but Falconi parried it away with the knife edge of his hand. But a long *tate no* blow caught the top of the American's left shoulder. His arm went numb and the straight *massuguna* jab hit his solar plexus.

Falconi went down, paralyzed and helpless. His perception far outstripped his physical abilities, and he watched in horrible fascination while Yoon raised the pole above his head to bring it down in a final, two-hand *chiheisen no* stroke that would split his skull.

Yoon took a deep breath, letting the power flow from his *hara*, up through his arms and into the pole to make it as integral a part of his being as the hands that held the weapon. Then, suddenly, the old Korean shuddered. He stepped back, his eyes glazing over. The staff dropped from his hands and Yoon fell to the ground, a long Vietnamese *phu nhan* dagger stuck deep between his shoulder blades.

Dinky Dow stepped out from the palm brush and went over to Yoon to retrieve his knife. He looked at his American friend and displayed a toothy, friendly grin.

'Hello, Falcon. What's happening?'

Major General Vang Ngoc stood in front of the map pinned to the wall of his headquarters hut. Obviously nervous, Major Dai Vo, commander of the 327th Infantry Battalion, and his commissar Major Hieu Lo Ren, stood not far from him.

The two had just briefed the general who, as commander of the Sixth Military Department, was in charge of the area the American raiders had been operating.

Vang was not an excitable man. The general had been in at the start of the Red Vietnamese's bid for a Communist take-over of their homeland. This struggle evolved into an ironic twist during World War II when the political aspects of the struggle took a back seat to fighting the Japanese. The Sons of Heaven, as they called themselves, had come into the country with the blessings of the Vichy government back in occupied France. At that time the American O.S.S. had provided men and supplies to aid the Reds in their fight against Nippon's aggression.

After that, beginning in 1946, he had participated in the eight-year war against the French. It was during these various conflicts that Vang had learned that patient plodding many times produced better results than exuberance and overconfidence. The report he had just received in the handling of the situation at Garrison Three had smacked most disturbingly of the latter two qualities.

The war against the French had been a fight against a modern European nation, but one that had dispatched an expeditionary force that bordered on being paupers. The French troops, volunteers, mercenaries and adventurers, had fought their good fight with a supply system fraught with mediocre equipment that had either been loaned to them, they had leased or been given as outright gifts.

Their strongest ally, the United States, had displayed a startling lack of interest in helping the French in their anti-Communist stand. The effort to stem the Red tide, clouded in a pseudo-cause of independence, had been vocally and repeatedly labeled as neo-colonialism by the political left wing of several western nations. No one seemed to bring up the point that the Vietnamese would exchange their French colonial masters for native-born puppets whose strings would be pulled by the Soviet Union.

Such a program of confusion requires time and the willingness to sacrifice one's own people by a carload if necessary. As a dedicated Communist, General Vang believed that if it took a bloodbath to gain one's goals – so be it!

The Americans who were beginning to step up their help of the South Vietnamese did not have that dedication – nor did their allies. The best way to take advantage of such a situation would be to kill as many as possible in a drawn-out conflict that would tax the patience of the United States public. Eventually they would demand that their leaders extricate them from an intolerable situation.

General Vang was a realist. He knew that if the Americans wanted to really kick Communist asses in Southeast Asia, they could. There was no way the North Vietnamese could ever *defeat* the USA. But there would be methods that could be employed that would make them *quit*.

And that could be claimed as a victory too.

Vang put his finger at a spot on the Mau Xanh River. 'This is your last contact with the imperialists?'

'Yes, Comrade, General,' Dai said. 'Then our air force massacred my men, and the Yankees escaped in the confusion.'

'But the pilots were closely and vigorously interrogated, Comrade Major,' Vang said. 'All three substantiate each other's story that the radio communications instructed them to change the procedures and make their strike on top of the bluffs.'

Hieu, feeling superior, interrupted cockily. 'There is obviously a display of great incompetency somewhere. I shall, of course, make a full report to party headquarters of my suspicions, Comrade General.'

Vang, an old survivor, gave Hieu a cold, threatening look. 'It is my opinion that most of the time when a unit performs badly, it is because their commissar failed to instill the proper devotion to socialism in the soldiers, thus making their fighting spirits less than effective in our noble struggle.'

Stark, staggering, undeniable fear quickly stabbed through Hieu's defensive, paranoic mind. 'But . . . but, Comrade General, the 327th fought bravely. It was not their courage that failed, it was the technology of the aircraft and the radio equipment that caused the terrible incident on the Mau Xanh.'

'Those were all manufactured in the glorious Soviet Union,' Vang reminded him enjoying the look of fear that had come across the commissar's face.

'Of course, the instruments were precise and meticulously constructed, Comrade General,' Hieu said. 'But the men who handled them lacked the necessary expertise.'

'Enough!' Vang exclaimed. 'I am in no mood to listen to rhetoric or excuses. The fact of this matter is that we must catch and destroy the raiders. As many as possible must be taken alive for trial and propaganda. Such a *coup* would enhance our efforts not only in Asia but in all parts of the world.'

'Yes, Comrade General!' both Dai and Hieu intoned.

'Now the Americans have more than an untried battalion looking for them,' Vang said indicating the area covered on the map by the Sixth Military Department. 'An entire division of our people's army is currently concentrating on the task of bringing them to justice.' He checked the approximate location of the invaders on the map. 'They must be in here somewhere. And that is too far from the south to avoid contact with our troops for very long. The proper placing and maneuvering of our soldiers will force the invaders into the exact place I wish them to be – with their backs to the Song Bo River.' He took his helmet off the desk behind him. 'And I shall personally take command of this effort.'

EIGHTEEN

Dinky Dow's return to the detachment caused a slight change in the re-organization. Sergeant Ray Limo was taken out of the Recon Element and put into Fire Team Alpha. The short Vietnamese lieutenant took his place.

And, besides the advantage of having regained an effective member of his unit, Dinky Dow provided another benefit. During the time he had called in the air strikes on the NVA position on the bluffs, he had pulled maps from the body of the young lieutenant he had killed there. They covered an area as far south as Da Nang in friendly territory, thus making it easy for Falconi to have a better idea of what lay ahead of them.

Sometimes ignorance is bliss and in that particular case, the old cliché was doubly true. The map shook the Falcon and his men somewhat by giving them undeniable knowledge they were far from home and that things might get worse before they got better.

The Black Eagles would now be following survival routines by living off the land and drinking untreated water when not able to boil any. The second evening away from the bluffs, before darkness set in, the ever concerned Malpractice McCorkel used the cookset in his medical equipment to boil up enough water to give each man a canteenfull. The stuff would only cool off to tepid, but it was still better than a case of typhoid.

Food wasn't that much of a problem. Not only were the men well versed in edible plants and animals in that part of the world, they were old soldiers, and knew enough before the mission to stick a little extra in their packs or pockets. Thus, cereal protein bars, small cans of fruits from Cs, packets of dried food, and other miscellaneous 'goodies' were available to them. Colonel Baldwin and Marvin Dayton were allowed to share in these small bounties, and their strength had continued to grow.

The air force pilot now toted an M16 and had been given some equipment from the KIAs. By helping guard Colonel Nguyen, he relieved another man for combat duty when needed. And some rudimentary instruction had made it possible for Baldwin to lend some volume to the detachment's fire power.

The small force fell into a routine of travel and wait – travel and wait – until the contact with the NVA patrol, which was as unexpected as it was vicious.

Archie Dobbs had tripped over the enemy point man. The guy, as good at the job as Archie, was a veteran who had scored the biggest advantage in jungle combat. He had perceived the opposition before they perceived him. Where he lacked Dobbs' expertise was in quick reaction. He hadn't even gotten the muzzle of the assault rifle up when the American's own weapon slapped two rounds into his head.

Then the tropical forest blew up.

Dinky Dow covered Dobbs' withdrawal, and the two turned and rushed back to link up with Fire Team Alpha. Ray Limo, the farthest man forward, helped them by cutting loose a few bursts in the general direction of the enemy. Two alert NVA riflemen, each as much a veteran as their point man, responded quickly. One of their rounds slammed into Limo's chest and the other took out a big hunk of deltoid muscle. The American grimaced and sank to one knee. Two more bullets sliced empty air above his head, but a third caught him full in the face and sent his lower jaw spinning off into the bushes.

Calvin Culpepper, his ebony face streaked with sweat, hurled a grenade. It went off six feet over the ground spraying out shrapnel that badly wounded one of the Reds and tore open the chest of the other. Calvin rushed up to where Ray Limo lay and gave him a quick checking out – that was all it took to see the man had been in his last fire fight.

Fire Team Alpha pulled back toward Master Sergeant Snow's Bravos, who set up a murderous covering fusillade until the others joined up with them. Next, both groups withdrew together under the screen of bullets thrown out by Marvin Dayton and Malpractice McCorkel. Colonel Baldwin and Bill Thompson hustled their prisoner on farther back where the recon element, now with Falconi, cut loose with their own volleys.

The remainder of the detachment joined them and the leapfrog withdrawal continued until contact had been broken with the NVA patrol.

General Vang Ngoc, sweat streaming down from his helmet, stood in the jungle and took the lieutenant's salute. 'How many casualties did you inflict on the enemy?' he asked.

'One, Comrade General,' the lieutenant said. 'I lost two men from a grenade and another was shot.'

'Show me on your map where this incident occurred,' Vang commanded.

The lieutenant unfolded the soiled cartograph and placed a soiled finger at a spot he had previously marked. 'Here, Comrade General. It is in the north of our patrol sector.'

'I see,' Vang said. 'Let's see . . . they were here –' He noted the location of the bluffs on the Mau Xanh River. '– and now they've reached this point and withdrew west, correct?'

'Yes, Comrade General,' the lieutenant affirmed.

'Then the *con de hoang* are between your unit on the east, the 418th Infantry on the west. To the north are the remnants of the 327th moving toward them,' General Vang said.

'And they want revenge badly,' the lieutenant added.

'I am counting on their shame and anger to hurry this affair to its natural conclusion,' Vang said. He looked at the map again. Then he laughed. 'The Americans are following my desires as if obeying operations orders issued by my headquarters. They will soon reach the Song Bo River to the south. They'll not cross that mighty stream like they did the Mau Xanh!'

'It is only a matter of time, Comrade General,' the lieutenant said.

'Now it is,' Vang agreed. 'We've got them locked in tighter than a virgin's *lo turcung!*'

Dinky Dow slowly pulled the pin on the grenade and held the firing handle down in a tight grip. He crawled forward a meter and stopped.

The NVA soldiers still talked softly among themselves. The smell of tea wafted gently from their small campfire.

The South Vietnamese finally reached the outer layer of

leaves and could see the three men. Obviously goofing off, they smoked cigarettes and watched their tea. Now and then one would get up and peer off in an easterly direction. That would be where their sergeant was, Dinky Dow told himself. He picked up a small stone and tossed it in the direction the soldiers seemed most concerned about. They all jumped up and peered fearfully over that way. Dinky Dow gave the grenade an underhand throw that carried it into the pan of boiling tea.

The three turned at the sound of the splash. One peered in at the liquid which now bubbled and hissed. '*Cai nay la cai gi?*' he asked.

Before he could get an answer, the grenade exploded. Shrapnel, bits of the pot and hot tea showered the trio of stragglers. Dinky Dow rushed into the impromptu camp and pulled the AK47s, bandoleers of ammo, grenades and equipment belts from the tree where they'd been so carefully hung.

Then the ex-VC melted back into the forest.

The Australian NCO, his beige beret bearing a winged dagger insignia, strode smartly up to the guard at the SOG headquarters gate and presented his ID and the document summoning him.

His khaki uniform was pressed and sharp, while the three chevrons surmounted by a crown on his sleeves identified him as a staff sergeant. The peculiar parachute insignia above the devices of rank and the badge on his headgear further marked him as a member of the SAS – the elite Special Air Service.

The guard directed him into the foyer of the building where he endured yet another expected scrutiny. A quick interior phone call produced an usher for him, and the tough looking Aussie was taken to the third floor of the building.

Clayton Andrews answered the knock on his office door with a curt, 'Come in!'

The Australian sergeant stepped inside. 'Mister Andrews?'

The CIA operative stood up and offered his hand. 'Yes. And you'll be Sergeant Newcomb, of course.'

'Yes, sir,' Newcomb said. 'My commander has informed me of this summons.' He dropped a message on Andrews' desk.

'Sit down, Sergeant Newcomb,' Andrews invited him. 'Can I

get you something to drink?'

'Scotch would be nice, sir. I take it straight.'

'Fine.' Clayton poured a generous glassful and handed it to the SAS man. Then he settled back once again into his chair behind the desk. 'I understand you've been on ops south of Dien Bien Phu.'

'Yes, sir.'

'We've got a problem out there that you might be able to help us with,' Andrews said.

'I'd be happy to try, sir.'

'We have a team in the area that is in dire need of extraction. They went out on a rescue mission that went bad from the start, I'm afraid. We've only confirmed their approximate whereabouts and what happened to them about two hours ago. And that from contact with Coteau-Vert tribesmen.'

'Yes, sir. They're my lot, you know. Rather primitive mountaineers, but quite bright. We've managed to use them for recce missions, a few raids and other operations as well as in setting up quite effective escape and evasion routes.'

'That's why we asked for you. We need someone who can go in there and link up with our guys and bring them out through the normal E and E net.'

'What is this . . . this approximate location you're speaking of, sir?' Newcomb asked.

'I'll show you on my map,' Andrews said. He got up and the Australian sergeant followed him to the wall. He pointed to a point slightly east of Dien Bien Phu. 'That's where they are, Sergeant Newcomb.'

'Bloody hell! North of the Song Bo River?'

'Yes.'

'Are they in contact with the NVA?' Sergeant Newcomb asked.

'It appears so – unfortunately,' Andrews answered.

'Impossible to get them out there, sir,' Newcomb said.

Andrews smiled and shrugged. 'Then I guess you're not interested in making the try.'

'Of course I am, sir,' Newcomb said seriously. 'It's only impossible – and the impossible doesn't take an SAS man over two or three days to accomplish.'

It was then that Andrews noticed the motto on Newcomb's beret badge:

WHO DARES WINS

Archie Dobbs performed a classical exhibition of the Georgia high step. He lifted his left knee up enough that the foot cleared any low bushes. He gently lowered it until his boot barely made contact with the soil beneath it. A soft bit of probing to make sure there were no twigs underneath to snap loudly nor dried vegetation to crackle, then he gradually let his full weight down on that foot.

He repeated the process with the opposite leg.

An hour of this, with Fire Team Bravo behind him, had resulted in not much ground covered, but at least the short distance traveled had been accomplished safely.

Suddenly Archie stopped and held up his hand to signal the others to do likewise. Master Sergeant John Snow, Sergeant First Class Jan Miskoski and Staff Sergeant Lightfingers O'Quinn froze. Not a muscle, other than blinking eyes, twitched among the trio. Archie raised his M16 above his head, and swung the muzzle forward. Then he turned and held out his hand to indicate the number five. He lowered it and raised it again, this time with one finger raised up.

Six NVA were ahead in the area indicated.

The three Bravos took an incredibly long time to draw up even with him. When they did, each had an opportunity to catch sight of the Red soldiers. The half dozen enemy troopers, evidently set up as an ambush or listening post, peered intently in the opposite direction.

Snow silently signaled each man his target, then raised his M16. The fire burst burped out in the dense vegetation. The back of the soldier directly in front of the top kick exploded four times in simultaneous little spurts of blood as the bullets stitched across him.

One NVA caught only one round, and that in the buttocks. He rolled over and worked the trigger of the AK47. Jan Miskoski flipped over on his back while O'Quinn finished off the North Vietnamese. A bullet in the throat did the job.

The marine rushed to examine Miskoski while his three companions hurried to the enemy bodies. They stripped them of weapons and ammo.

O'Quinn re-joined his comrades. 'Jan's had it,' he said curtly.

Snow turned from the task of stripping the equipment from the enemy dead and went to the body, kneeling down for a close, but unnecessary examination. The Chicago sergeant, his face mangled beyond recognition with only the open eyes recognizable, stared up in unperceiving death at the trees above.

'Hell of a shame,' the top NCO said.

'Ain't they all?' Archie Dobbs remarked.

The team sergeant got to his feet. He made sure everyone had loaded up. 'Let's go.'

The scene in the jungle, which had burst forth in violence only moments before, was now as quiet as the seven bodies that lay sprawled in the bloody vegetation.

General Vang Ngoc took the written report and perused the document carefully. As he read, his features gradually assumed a wide smile. Finally, with an air of happy triumph, he flung the paper to the field desk in the tent.

'Ah! The Americans are now taking weapons and ammunition from our dead!' the general exclaimed. 'When such wealthy wastrels begin to exhibit symptoms of thrift and miserliness it means but one thing – they are running short of supplies.'

'I would not think such a thing is possible,' his adjutant marveled. 'Even the South Vietnamese are beginning to waste material since their attachment to the Yankees is growing abundantly with each passing week.'

'This will be better than fighting the French in the good old days,' Vang said. 'Those *can de hoang* were used to going without. This situation should prove quite demoralizing for our affluent opponents.'

The adjutant nodded in satisfaction. 'Do you think the decadent capitalist swine will crumble in the face of deprivation?'

'Of course!' Vang crowed. 'Perhaps if we got a loudspeaker and offered them hamburgers they would crawl in to us without our having to hunt for them anymore.'

* * *

Staff Sergeant Marvin Dayton, the ex-POW, was taken from the Prisoner Detail and transferred to Fire Team Bravo to make up for the loss of SFC Jan Miskoski.

Lightfingers O'Quinn was forced back into supply work. With the shortage of 5.56 millimeter ammo for the M16s, he had to collect it all up and give it to the Team Alpha. Master Sergeant Snow's team, along with the prisoner detail, now carried Soviet AK47s with bandoleers taken from dead NVA.

The last of the American grenades had been the one Lieutenant Dinky Dow used to flavor the tea being brewed by the trio of luckless Reds earlier in the day. Of the eighteen grenades now in possession of the detachment, the Recon Element had four; Fire Team Alpha, six; Fire Team Bravo, six; and Captain Robert Falconi had attached two to his patrol harness.

Although these were Soviet designed defensive grenades, designated as Type F-1 by the Russians, they had been manufactured in Czechoslovakia. They had a delay type fuse and a fragmentation radius of fourteen meters.

The Black Eagles bore the explosive devices no ill-will because of their origin, however, and would gladly throw any grenade, regardless of country of manufacture or design, at any Communist soldier regardless of his race, religion or national origin. Any enemy of freedom, despite his ethnic background, could expect to be shot or blown to hell with the same degree of prejudice he demonstrated toward democracies.

The Black Eagles were equal opportunity killers.

The Falcon ran a quick check on his men to make sure all were as well equipped as could possibly be managed. The commander of the Black Eagles had a deep undeniable feeling in his gut that they were being systematically and relentlessly driven into a corner. Every soldierly instinct he had screamed an alarm at him.

Well, maybe it don't look real good, his mind told him, *but what the hell? Nobody said this job was gonna be easy!*

He turned to Archie Dobbs and Dinky Dow. 'Okay, big recon team, let's move 'em out!'

NINETEEN

Captain Robert Falconi instinctively ducked at the sudden gush of gunfire up toward the front of the column.

Ritchie Wakely's Alphas went left and hit the dirt, while Top's Bravos took the right of the column. Back at the Prisoner Detail, Malpractice McCorkel knocked Colonel Nguyen to the ground. The NVA officer, his hands cuffed behind him, slammed face-first into the dirt. Both Lieutenant Bill Thompson and Lieutenant Colonel Winston Baldwin covered the rear of the detachment.

Within moments Archie Dobbs and Dinky Dow raced back through the jungle and joined their commanding officer. 'NVA – lots of 'em!' Dobbs said between breaths.

'Maybe a battalion,' Dinky Dow added.

'Okay,' Falconi said. 'We'll pull back and hold fast. In the meantime, you two head to the east and see what's there.'

The Black Eagles, covering each other, moved cautiously back the way they had come to avoid contact with the approaching enemy. The Recon Element's mission didn't take them long. They were back within a quarter of an hour – with more bad news.

'Two rifle companies, reinforced to the east, Skipper,' Dobbs reported. 'And another battalion on our north.'

'Well!' Falconi said in pseudo jocularity. 'That saves me the trouble of having to figure out which way to go, doesn't it? We'll have to pull back south.'

'One problem, Falcon,' Dinky Dow interjected. 'The Song Bo is that way. Big, big fucking river.'

'We'll have to check out that situation more carefully when we get there,' the Falcon said. 'Well – as I've said so many times in this operation – let's get the fuck outta here!'

The detachment formed a single skirmish line, with flankers out for security, to make the slow, careful backward-stepping withdrawal from the large units that were pressing down on them.

Falconi wasn't fooling himself. The bastards knew where they were. Unless the fucking North Vietnamese Army was made up of the blind-and-deaf, there was no way they could not have virtually ringed in the Black Eagles. The enemy may not have been able to absolutely pin-point their location, but they knew enough to be able to herd the Americans in any direction they desired.

More gunfire blasted out on the right flank.

Within moments, Ritchie Wakely, Horny Galchaser and Calvin Culpepper appeared. The young lieutenant's face clearly showed the strain they were under. 'They made contact with us, Falcon,' he said. 'We tried to delay 'em, but –'

'It's okay, Ritchie,' Falcon told him. 'Keep on the right, we'll do the best we can.'

The pressure kept up until all the Black Eagles teams were in visual contact with each other. In a couple of instances, the men were pressed so close together they bumped into each other.

Colonel Nguyen Chi Roi, former master and commandant of Garrison Three, had conducted himself as a sullen, barely cooperative prisoner during their days of flight. Now he became vocal, his derisive laughter mocking and insulting. He moved awkwardly because of his shackled hands, but he didn't seem to notice the discomfort any more. 'You will die soon, Yankees. Or I will have you under my tender care in Garrison Three.'

'You motherfucker!'

Marvin Dayton's temper snapped and he rushed from his place in Bravo Team's skirmish line, bowled over Malpractice McCorkel and shoved the muzzle of the AK47 into the NVA officer's face. 'Suck it, you bastard!'

Nguyen stared at him incredulously.

'I said suck it!' Dayton snarled. He shoved the weapon forward so hard it cut Nguyen's mouth. 'Take the goddamned thing in your mouth, you bastard!'

Nguyen reluctantly parted his lips. The weapon was thrust into his mouth.

'If those cocksuckers get in close at all,' Dayton said, 'I'm pulling this trigger. If it's the last fucking thing I do, I'm gonna splatter your fucking brains all over this stinking jungle, Nguyen. Do you understand? *Do you!*'

Nguyen nervously nodded his head to indicate that he, most certainly, knew what the American sergeant meant.

Falconi, while appreciating Dayton's rather destructive attitude toward the NVA, felt he should caution him. 'A very important part of our mission,' he said, 'is to get this guy back to our boys in the CIA.'

'If you leave him to me, sir,' Dayton said coldly. 'I can guarantee the colonel here will be looking forward to talking with them. In fact, he'll be begging to!'

'I suppose,' Falconi conceded.

'It's sort of like the night my dad and brothers and I caught a burglar in the house,' Dayton said with a cold smile. 'Before we finished with him, he was pleading for the cops.'

'Did you turn the bastard over to them?' Falconi asked.

'There's a spot in our flower garden where the plants bloom quite a bit more than anywhere else in the backyard,' Dayton said.

'Saved the old hometown from spending money on a trial, right?' Falcon said.

'And a few more houses from being burglarized and probably somebody from being murdered too,' Dayton said.

'You folks performed a good deed,' the Falcon remarked.

'Oh, yes, sir!' Dayton said. He glared at Nguyen. 'We like doing good deeds.'

A rapid rolling firefight broke out along the line. It increased in volume until a few stray rounds splattered in the trees around them.

'Looks like things are closing in on us now,' Falconi said. He could see both fire teams had been forced in even tighter. He grabbed Dinky Dow. 'See what we've got behind us.'

'Right, Falcon.' The little ARVN officer took off through the bushes.

Small arms fire, both semi and full automatic, broke out again. This time there was a marked increase in incoming rounds.

Suddenly three heavily camouflaged NVA broke into view spraying steel-jacketed rounds from their Russian PPS-43 submachine guns. Ritchie Wakely staggered back, spun and fell to the ground. His torso was hamburger.

Horny Galchaser swept the small attack team with his M16, knocking them sprawling in a tangle of palm fronds. 'Damn!' he spat. 'All we need now. Suicide attacks for Chrissake!'

'Falcon! Falcon!' Dinky Dow's high pitch voice sounded above the fighting. 'The Song Bo is only twenty meters behind us.'

'Right,' Falconi said. 'Take over the Alphas. Ritchie's bought the farm.'

'Right, Falcon!' The Vietnamese officer went forward the scant distance necessary to join Horny Galchaser and Calvin Culpepper.

The Black Eagles, involved in purely defensive firing now, kept the growing numbers of attackers at bay while they stumbled back.

Finally there was no place to go.

'Find spots with good fields of fire,' Falconi said. 'Team Leaders, turn on those Prick-Sixes.' He wanted the radios in operation since voice commands, even in that confined space, would be impossible with so many weapons firing at once.

Dayton, with his weapon still in Nguyen's mouth, swung the NVA around. He spoke to the Falcon without taking his eyes off the prisoner. 'Now, sir?'

'Get back to your team,' Falcon ordered. 'When the time comes I'll off the little bastard.'

'Yes, sir.' Dayton reluctantly left Nguyen and went forward to join the others on the firing line.

Nguyen watched the American NCO return to his fire team. He spat. 'Bah! You are all doomed!' He glared at Falconi. 'The only chance you have of avoiding imminent death is to surrender to me. Captain Falconi. Tell your men to drop their arms and I shall take care of the rest. I can get my comrades to stop firing if you follow my instructions explicitly.'

'You're about to come face-to-face with the undeniable fact of you and your kind's incredible stupidity,' Falcon said. 'If we were fighting a civilized enemy and were hemmed in and outnumbered like this, I would probably raise a white flag for a bit of negotiating, then honorably surrender and be marched away to receive treatment according to the Geneva Convention. But if we give up to you jack-offs, we're facing ungodly years of mistreatment, deprivation and whatever other miseries you could devise for us. Sort of takes the attraction out of that possible course of action, doesn't it?'

'Then you'll die!' Nguyen exclaimed.

'And more of your soldiers will die too,' Falconi countered.

'Ha!' Nguyen snarled. 'That bothers us not in the least.'

'The difference between you and us,' Falconi said. 'And if you have no more consideration for your own people than that, what the hell can we expect from you? And that includes your form of government, asshole.'

'A good soldier is always prepared to die,' Nguyen said. 'I am ready now – this moment – to give my life for my cause.'

'Hell, you might as well,' Falconi said. 'If they ever get you back they'll put you through the fucking mill and you know it. Besides, you ignorant bastard, you don't know any better. If you weren't such a no good son of a bitch, I'd feel sorry for you.'

A rapid increase in the firing heralded an attack. The NVA troops in the center – the Black Eagles' old nemesis the 327th Infantry – launched a furious charge at their positions. Major Dai Vo, his Russian Tokarev pistol barking in the midst of the roar of assault rifles, moved in with the lead squads. Not so much out of patriotic or vengeful fervor, but because General Vang Ngoc had put him there.

The Black Eagles, firing short fire bursts, swept the brown clad figures in front of them, sending them toppling to the soft jungle ground. Dai, screaming in rage now, no longer gave a damn. Everything he'd worked for in the party and the army had gone up in smoke during the previous few days. He leaped over a duo of fallen NVA and ran toward the Americans.

Culpepper and O'Quinn, close together now that team integrity was gone, cut loose on the enemy officer. Dai, determined to take someone with him, took two hits but only stumbled sideways under the impact. He managed to get a few more paces forward when another round slapped him hard in the side. He spun around and fell to his knees facing rearward toward his own men. He collapsed onto his back, getting a distorted, upside down view of the Black Eagles' position. His last physical action was a desperate jerk on the trigger of the pistol, then he died in the undignified position of a whore waiting for a line of customers to mount her.

The bullet he fired zipped low across the ground, snipping blades of grass and smacked into Lieutenant Bill Thompson's forehead. Its trajectory was altered by the sudden impact and the round continued upward out of the top of his skull, flipping a hunk of scalp down over his face.

Lieutenant William Thompson, MD and US Navy SEAL, with generations of scientific and medical tradition behind him, died but ten yards from the peasant who had fired the fatal shot in a sporadic jerk of dying muscles.

Winston Baldwin, USAF, had experienced having friends killed in war before. But they'd been pilots whose bodies had been unseen, lost entities. The only evidence of their deaths had been written reports and empty bunks in the Bachelor Officers Quarters of some air base. This time he could not only see the bloody cadaver, but had some of his brains splattered in his face.

He screamed in rage and pumped bullets into the dead NVA officer who had slain Bill Thompson.

'Hey, goddamnit!' Archie Dobbs behind him yelled grabbing his hand to stop the shooting. 'Save some of that fucking ammo for the live ones!'

A brief lull occurred in which Dinky Dow turned over the leadership of Alpha Team to Horny Galchaser. Since he had been doing most of his fighting with Archie Dobbs, he decided to stick with him now – right to the bitter fucking end.

Now, as ever, demonstrating his courage, the feisty little Vietnamese crawled forward into the enemy dead and returned with ammo and some more grenades.

Within moments another attack was launched. Screaming NVA came at them in a pincer movement. Master Sergeant John Snow, Lightfingers O'Quinn and Marvin Dayton swept a half-circle area in front of them. The Communist soldiers, urged on by their shrieking commissars behind them, ran blindly and stupidly into the fusillade. They fell in piles, others leaping over the mounds of dead comrades to catch the 7.63 millimeter slugs in their own bodies as they added to the growing number of enemy dead.

Archie Dobbs and Dinky Dow had too much pressure on their

part of the line. Despite firing as rapidly as possible, several determined Reds reached them. Archie threw a horizontal butt-stroke that felled the first man to reach him, but the second bowled him over. Dinky Dow took out one man with a slashing bayonet attack, shot the one about to bash out Archie's brains, then turned and grabbed the next exuberant attacker by an arm and hurled him over his shoulder. Before the Communist could regain his feet, Dinky Dow put two quick shots into his back.

'Let's get the hell outta here!' Archie yelled scrambling back to a standing position. 'We gotta shorten this fucking line, we're too spread out for mass attacks.'

Without knowing it, he was echoing the same orders that Falconi at that very moment was yelling into the mouthpiece of his Prick-Six Radio. Horny Galchaser having taken impromptu command on Dinky Dow's order, now held the Alpha Team's commo gear. Master Sergeant Snow, without taking time to affirm having received the order, got his own team backpedaling quickly toward the rear.

This maneuver left a vacuum in the battle area that was quickly filled by the ever pressing NVA troops. The Reds fired blindly in the direction of the retreating Americans.

Marvin Dayton took several hits in the torso, his tiger fatigues instantly soaked in blood before his lifeless cadaver hit the ground.

Minutes later, literally under Falconi's nose, the entire detachment formed up. The Song Bo River's bank was only a meter from where they stood. Every man looked at their commander, but not one suggested surrender.

Falconi was proud of them and loved every one of the guys there. They had reached the proverbial situation of having no quarter and offering none.

The captain grinned at the survivors and winked, his voice strong despite the fear and anger gnawing at his gut.

'Kick ass!'

TWENTY

'Here they come!'

Archie Dobbs' voice sounded above the preliminary shots of the new attacks on this final, small position. The Black Eagles, blocked in the back by the wide and deep Song Bo, and in front by a regimental-sized enemy attack force, prepared to make the NVA pay dearly for this victory.

What really bothered them was the knowledge that their bodies, and any survivors, would be paraded out for eastern bloc news photographers whose pictures would end up in American publications for their families and friends to see.

Almost shoulder to shoulder, the detachment put out a rate of fire that swept the first two waves of attackers off their feet. The ones behind hesitated, sustaining a fair loss in their own ranks, then tried to pull back. Screaming officers beat and pummeled these men forward until they, too, were mowed down to join comrades already sprawled out in front of the American positions.

Colonel Nguyen, at one point, leaped up and tried to run for the Communist lines, but Falconi tackled him and dragged the shrieking fanatic back to the interior of the American's impromptu last stand.

Again the NVA swept forward. This time the Falcon's men hurled a pre-planned barrage of grenades that fell among the attacking enemy. The explosives detonated almost simultaneously, creating an instantaneous curtain of steel that shredded the enemy's forward rank. Those farther behind, including the lightly wounded, stumbled and staggered through the maze of cadavers to face the chillingly accurate fire of the Black Eagles. A few, lucky enough to have been missed initially, stood up and tried to trade individual shots with the Black Eagles, but they dropped one by one.

And the pressure continued.

It was obvious the North Vietnamese commander was going

all the way on this one. There were no breaks between units. He had massed his men and driven them forward. If they couldn't outshoot the American raiders, then they would literally crush them with their numbers.

Falconi kept his eye on Nguyen, deciding to wait until the last minute to use the wily colonel. What better way than to pick up the little bastard and run at the enemy? There would be th short-lived, but undeniable satisfaction of seeing the son of a bitch die under his own side's bullets before the Falcon bought the farm himself.

Bullets zipped and whined in the inaccurate, hasty fire directed at them. Falconi had hit the dirt, his head near his radio, returning fire over Nguyen's trembling body. He noted a break in the hissing noise of the receiver. He looked around to see which one of his men would be attempting to raise him on the net – and why – but none had their commo gear in operation. Perhaps it was the NVA, but how would they know what frequency or crystal to use?

He picked up the Prick-Six. 'This is Black Eagle, over.'

The voice, accented and clear as a bell, came back.

'Black Eagle. This is Aussie. What has Raggedy Andy got that you ain't got? Over.'

For one incredulous moment, Falconi stared at the radio. The proper code of contact was as unbelievable as it was unexpected. He shook himself into action to give the correct answer. 'Aussie, this is Black Eagle. Cotton balls. Over.'

'Roger, Black Eagle. *Duck!* Over.'

Despite not knowing what the strange voice meant, Falconi knew better than to hesitate. 'Cease firing!' he yelled. 'Get down! Get down! Kiss dirt, goddamnit!'

His men, as conditioned as he, did exactly that.

The first mortar rounds dropped in. One long and the other, causing a bit of nervous consternation, fell into the river behind them. But the third was on target. Then the fourth, fifth, sixth, and the others that followed.

'Black Eagle, this is Aussie. Boats crossing for you. Meet 'em in the middle of the bleedin' river. Out.'

No more transmission, no more questions. Falconi grabbed Nguyen's collar and headed for the water, yelling the motto of the United States Infantry School over his shoulder:

'*Follow Me!*'

He hit the water and turned to see Malpractice McCorkel behind him. The medic was cheerfully inquisitive. 'What the fuck's going on, Falcon?'

Falconi turned Nguyen over to him. 'Take this little creep with you. Whoever you see out there, do exactly what he tells you.'

'Right!' Swimming clumsily, Malpractice took his burden out with him.

Colonel Baldwin came up next with Archie Dobbs and Dinky Dow. Falconi sent him into the water and had the two members of the Recon Element stay with him to give covering fire.

Horny Galchaser and Calvin Culpepper were next into the river. Lightfingers O'Quinn made a quick appearance with Master Sergeant John Snow on his tail.

The Falcon, Dobbs and Dinky Dow cut loose on the NVA who first appeared on the river bank they had just evacuated. These early-comers paid for their eagerness with their lives. Others behind them also tumbled under the lead of the three men to add their corpses to the hill of other dead NVA in the area. But the supporting skirmishers were right behind them, and the added fire power turned the tables. There was no stopping them now.

Shots zapped at the remaining Black Eagles, kicking up spurts of dirt and splashing in the water. Snow grunted and pitched forward into O'Quinn's arms.

'Get him the fuck outta here!' Falcon yelled. He and his two cohorts fired their last rounds at the exact moment the mortar barrage crept back to the river bank. The 60 millimeter shells obliterated the scene with roaring, multiple explosions that flung pieces of North Vietnamese soldiers into the river.

Then the remainder of the Black Eagles swam out into the sweeping current of the Song Bo.

Rubber boats filled with strange looking savages were in the middle of the river. These small, exotic men wearing loin cloths but carrying M16s, reached into the water and pulled the survivors aboard while shells continued to pound the shore that had just been evacuated.

When they reached the far side, Falconi stumbled ashore. A

figure standing there, wearing tiger fatigues, gave the captain one of the sharpest salutes he had ever received.

'Sir! Sergeant Newcomb, Australian SAS reporting!'

Glancing behind the non-commissioned officer, Falcon saw three more Australians, all manning a small battery of mortars with several of their strange primitive friends helping them. He grinned wearily at the Aussie. 'You know, *Waltzing Matilda* has always been one of my favorite songs!'

TWENTY-ONE

Falconi looked out the door of the descending H34 helicopter and saw Clayton Andrews standing just off the landing pad of the B Camp. The CIA operative turned his head to avoid the swirling dust kicked up by the aircraft's rotors.

The Falcon jumped out first then turned to help Lightfingers O'Quinn and Malpractice McCorkel unload the poncho shrouded body. The rest of the passengers disembarked: Lieutenant Colonel Winston Baldwin, SFC Horny Galchaser, SGT Calvin Culpepper, and finally Archie Dobbs and Dinky Dow with Colonel Nguyen between them. All hurried across the pad with Falconi following. He stopped and nodded to Andrews.

'Glad that we got out as many as we did at least,' Andrews said. He looked at the dead man. 'Who's that?'

'The Top,' Falconi answered.

'Damn!' It was an exclamation more of grief than anger. He noted Colonel Nguyen Chi Roi, still handcuffed, being escorted away by Horny Galchaser and Calvin Culpepper. 'I take it you weren't able to get the North Korean.'

'Oh, we got the wily old fox all right,' Falconi said. 'And he damn near beat the shit out of me before Dinky Dow did him in with that curvy dagger of his.'

'I presume you'll fill in the juicy details on your debriefing,' Andrews said. 'I'm glad to see you got Baldwin out though. I presume that Special Forces sergeant was also in no shape for liberation.'

'He was ready,' the Falcon said. 'In fact they were fattening him up for some propaganda ploy or other. But we lost him in the final firefight.'

'Under the circumstances, you and the guys did a superlative job,' Andrews said.

The first chopper took off and the second came in. This time Sergeant Newcomb, the other SAS men and several of their native friends leaped off and hurried over to them. The Australian saluted Falconi. 'I only wish we could have gotten to you sooner, sir. We pushed things as best we could, but when one must deal solely with informers and recce patrols, it does take a bit o' time.'

'Your efforts are very well appreciated, believe me,' Falconi said sincerely.

'Well, I must tend to my report. We've paperwork in the Australian forces too, y'know.'

'Right,' Falconi said. He watched the SAS man head down to the camp with his strange comrades following.

'Who are those natives with the Australians?' Falconi asked.

'They're from the Coteau-Vert,' Andrews answered. 'A Montagnard bunch. They're more anti-Vietnam than anti-Communist, unfortunately.'

'In other words, they'll fight north or south with equal fervor?' Falconi asked.

'Yeah. Except our side has been giving them plenty of money and weapons, so they're content to shoot to the north,' Andrews said.

'Mercenary or not, they're mean little bastards and I'm glad they're on our side one way or the other,' Falconi said.

'How many personnel did you lose altogether?' Andrews asked.

'Counting everybody – thirteen guys – thirteen damned good guys,' Falconi said. 'How come we weren't told about that fucking battalion being in the vicinity of Garrison Three? That was what fucked everything all up.'

'We've only just learned that they arrived a day before you did,' Andrews explained. 'It's shitty, but one of those things. We think they were slated for duty down south, so maybe your hurting them turned out to be a blessing after all.'

'*C'est la guerre*, as Dutch Hosteins would say,' Falconi remarked. 'Another good man wasted.'

'Yeah,' Andrews agreed. 'Looks like he won't make it to the States after all.'

'What's going to be said to his brother?'

Andrews shrugged. 'I don't know – killed by terrorists, or something. The Vietnamese police will take care of informing the French Embassy.'

'We ought to write the guy's brother,' Falconi said.

'Forget it. We're not even supposed to know Bruno Hosteins existed, get it? We contact his family in New Jersey and they'll get curious,' Andrews said.

'What if I said I hung out in his bar?' Falconi suggested. 'I could write a letter to substantiate whatever the version the local cops give on his death. Then say he was a hell of a good guy, well liked with lots of friends – and all that. Might make his family feel a little better knowing there were others that thought a lot of him.'

'No.'

'Right.'

Andrews turned and Falconi followed him down the hill. The army captain looked around at the Special Forces B camp, fortified and well laid out that stretched before them. 'We gonna be debriefed here before R&R?'

'You're going to be debriefed here, yes,' Andrews said. 'But no R&R.'

Falconi stopped in mid-stride. 'Why the fuck not?'

'Another mission's popped up, and can't be put off,' Andrews said as they resumed their stroll to the installation's headquarters.

'Put somebody else on it, goddamnit it!'

'There's nobody else that can handle this baby,' Andrews said. 'As a matter of fact, the Australian is going in with you on this one.'

'I'm sure the guy's hardcore and all that, but these men of mine need a fucking break, Andy!'

'Sorry.'

Again Falconi stopped. 'What could be so goddamned important that these jokers of mine can't have some time off?'

Andrews looked back at him. 'How about a Soviet nuclear reactor in Laos?' He continued on his way down the hill.

Falconi stood there watching him, seething with anger. Then his emotions leveled off and he cooled down.

What the hell? Nobody said this job was going to be easy.

The heroic and unforgettable saga of one man's rise to military glory

Man of War

JOHN MASTERS

Bestselling author of THE LOSS OF EDEN trilogy

Captain Bill Miller is a modern MAN OF WAR.

This is his story – a huge, enthralling adventure of a soldier of our times, living and fighting through most of the major battles of this century.

Miller's career spans both World Wars and half the globe; from the General Strike and Indian Independence, to the Spanish Civil War and Dunkirk . . . For over twenty years, the unorthodox son of a shopkeeper learns his craft against the explosive panorama of international history. And there are other hostilities to suffer too – two marriages lost to ambition and dedication; alienation from fellow soldiers for his tactical part in Franco's victory. Whatever the price, Miller paid in full, for those moments of glory on the beaches of Dunkirk . . .

A monumental epitaph to a bestselling, masterly genius, MAN OF WAR is the last great story from the major war writer, the novel that only John Masters could write.

'Brilliant . . . packed with pace and detail . . . a splendid storyteller and a master at describing battles and campaigns.' *Daily Telegraph.*

FICTION 0 7221 5877 7 £2.50

Maj-Gen John Frost

2 PARA FALKLANDS

2 Para – the Second Battalion of the Parachute Regiment – fought at the heart of all the major battles in the Falklands. This is their story – the landing at San Carlos Water, the battles of Darwin, Goose Green, Fitzroy, Bluff Cove, Wireless Ridge and Stanley . . .

Written by one of 2 Para's most distinguished former commanders, who had privileged access not only to official daily records of the campaign, but also to the opinions of officers and ordinary soldiers, 2 PARA FALKLANDS is a soldier's account of a soldier's war. It is also a gripping adventure, and a powerful, moving testament to the courage and humanity of all those who gave their lives in the War, revealing the truth which has never been told by the numerous journalists who followed the Army to the Falklands.

'Splendidly told . . . blending the high emotion, the minor as well as the major heroisms, the humour, compassion and sheer courage of the soldiers who fought . . .' *Daily Telegraph*.

WAR NON-FICTION 0 7221 36897 £1.95